SINGLE

Single

MARGARET CLARKSON

KINGSWAY PUBLICATIONS
EASTBOURNE

First British edition 1980

First published in the USA by Harold Shaw Publishers under the title *So You're Single!*

ISBN 0 86065 076 6

Printed in Great Britain for
KINGSWAY PUBLICATIONS LTD
Lottbridge Drove, Eastbourne, E. Sussex BN23 6NT by
Richard Clay (The Chaucer Press) Ltd, Bungay, Suffolk

Contents

TO MY MARRIED FRIENDS
whose love and friendship have so enriched my life

Foreword

When a sensitive and intelligent woman poet writes about being single and the love that could not be, you might expect anything but common sense. Yet common sense is what Margaret Clarkson gives us — helpful common sense.

She brushes nothing under the carpet. Loneliness, bitterness, bewilderment, envy, eroticism, depression, the need for roots and the need for friendship are among the many themes she scrutinizes quietly and dispassionately. She shares her personal struggles with no hint of exhibitionism and presents solutions which are time-tested.

It is refreshing to read a book on such a theme which is free from both cheap psychological jargon and religious mush. In place of the latter, Miss Clarkson offers godliness, pointing us to the twin stars of God's sovereignty and his goodness. She does not permit herself or us the enervating luxury of self-pity, but reminds us that difficult roads are not impossible ones, and that solid rewards await those who tread them.

But this book is more than a call to courage. The later chapters are filled with hints and practical suggestions worked out in her years of being single. They give touching and amusing insights into what it is to be single, insights that will reassure the single person and open the eyes of those who are married. She sharply challenges both the insensitive behaviour of some married people and the myths about singleness they cherish. She also makes discerning suggestions to the church.

And unobtrusively she remains a poet to the end of the book, displaying a poet's gift of perception, and presenting truth in such a way that it convinces and moves us.

John White
Associate Professor of Psychiatry,
The University of Manitoba

Introduction

Why would anyone write a book about being single?

Why, indeed!

Today's young people are asking questions about the single state. Contemplating Christian mission, they are realizing that if they obey Christ's command, being single may well be part of their cost of discipleship. They are aware of the implications of being single as no other generation has ever been. They know what the world has to say about the matter; they want to know what God has to say. They want to talk with single Christians who know God's sufficiency. If some of us older single people don't speak up and tell them that God is greater than human need and that he is faithful, who will?

Nobody wants to be the one to open up a discussion about being single, and that included me. But God began to put pressure on me through a series of curious circumstances that had to be more than coincidence, at the same time backing it up by his own inward leading. I felt impelled to speak, even though it was against my natural inclination.

Much to my surprise, writing this book has been a beautiful and blessed experience, and one that I wouldn't have missed. Looking back on well over forty years of adulthood, all of them single, I am overwhelmed with wonder and worship as I trace God's hand at work in my life. I marvel, not at the poverty or emptiness that has been mine, but at the wealth of my satisfactions and joy. With David I exclaim, "Thou preparest a table before me in the presence of mine enemies; thou anointest my head with oil; my cup runneth over. Surely goodness and mercy shall follow me all the days of my life, and I will dwell in the house of the Lord for ever."

I hope that married as well as single people will read this book. If the church is truly to function as the body of Christ, it is important that married people know how single people think and feel. Because married people were all single once, they tend to think that they know all there is to know about being single. I suggest that this is not so; that there is a vast difference between being single at 25 or 30, with marriage still a viable possibility, and being single at 45 or 50 or 60, with little or no prospect of ever being anything else. Being single has a cumulative effect on the human spirit such that being single at 50 is entirely different from being single at 30.

Nor do I see widows and divorced people as single, although they may be alone. Single parents are still parents. Theirs is a problem of aloneness, not singleness. Yet we have certain problems in common which married people do not share and of which many of them are unaware. If we Christians are really to understand one another well enough to function as one, some of these things should be known.

When Christian was crossing the River at the close of *Pilgrim's Progress*, his heart failed him for fear. He began to sink in the cold, dark waters. But Hopeful, his companion, helped him to stand, calling out loudly, "Be of good cheer, my brother; I feel the bottom, and it is good." Then Christian recovered his faith, and passed safely through the waters to the Celestial City.

If there are single people who find the waters of singleness dark and deep, who feel, "I sink in deep waters; the billows go over my head; all his waves go over me," this is my message to you: "Be of good cheer, my brother, my sister; I feel the bottom, and it is good."

This book is a shout of triumph and praise to Jesus Christ, *El Shaddai*, the God Who Is Enough. His grace is sufficient for the deepest needs of the human heart. Trust him, for he is faithful.

1
Inquisition

It was my thirtieth birthday. I was spending the weekend in the home of friends whose fascinating children were among my greatest delights.

"What's it feel like to be thirty, Margie?" The thirteen-year old redhead beside me spoke suddenly as we stood at the mirror putting grips in our hair at bedtime.

"Not any different than it felt to be twenty," I replied lightly. "What questions kids do ask!" I smiled to myself inwardly.

Mary lifted wide amber eyes and looked deeply into mine.

"Margie," she inquired pensively, "don't you wish you had a man to kiss at night?"

I did an inward double-take. But ten years of teaching had taught me to register no surprise at any child's question, no matter what my private reaction. They had also taught me the futility of evasion. There was just no use in beating about the bush with this clear-eyed young lady who had been my friend all her life. And nothing from anyone as utterly transparent as Mary could possibly hurt me. There was no sting to her question, only a profound need to know. I drew a deep breath.

But without waiting for my reply, Mary was hastening on. "I have one, of course," she reflected happily, her face lighting up with a smile. "In fact, I have several of them." Her eyes softened at the thought of the men in her life — Daddy, Uncle John, Uncle Bill, Grandad. Then, with a little sigh, she came back to the point. "You haven't anyone, have you? Don't you wish you had?"

"I don't know that I've thought of it in just that way, Mary," I responded slowly, "but I know what you mean, all right."

"*Don't* you wish you had?" she persisted relentlessly.

"Yes, Mary," I answered, truthfully if somewhat reluctantly, "I suppose I do."

Looking up into my face, Mary smiled again, a slow, mysterious smile.

"I think every woman does," she murmured softly. Then, briskly, she concluded, "Not very many of us are willing to admit it, though!"

Over thirty years have passed since that night. Mary came to see the wisdom of restricting her nocturnal embraces and found her one special man to kiss at night. She must have kissed him well, for they have six children.

My single status has not changed. I think back to Mary's question, and smile. Such an interrogation would shake me less today than it did then. Today it is easier to express our feelings about such things than it used to be. A great deal more is known about human sexuality. We no longer feel slightly ashamed, nor even particularly shy, about acknowledging the human desires with which we have been created in the image of God. Not everything about the sexual revolution has been bad!

Yet thousands of us must live for years, even a lifetime, denied any opportunity to express our sexuality in the beauty and intimacy of Christian marriage. What God seems to give almost universally, sometimes he withholds.

How do such people fare in the face of human needs like that expressed by Mary's question? What answers does God give us when our hearts cry out to him? For there are answers. God would not be true to his nature or his name if, having promised to supply all his children's needs, he then proceeded to ignore the human needs of large numbers of them.

But God is true to himself. He does fulfil the needs of those who come to him. He does have answers for those who are prepared to seek them with diligence. God does not mock his children; he answers them, individually, intimately.

And that is what this book is all about.

2
Why Are There Single People?

Why, in a world so obviously designed for mating, should there be single people? Admittedly, some lower forms of life do not mate, but the higher one looks in the created order the more pronounced the mating instinct is seen to be. "God created man in his own image, in the image of God he created him; male and female he created them," we read in Genesis 1:27. Thus God made man, male and female, neither complete alone, each needing the other for true self-knowledge, self-affirmation and self-fulfilment.

Why, then, does the blight of being single rest upon so many? Why the thousands who for a variety of reasons find themselves unable to marry? Does God create his children to live in one way, only to force great numbers of them to live in another, lesser way? How many times has this question been asked! How easy it is to blame God for my being single!

But we forget. We do not live in the perfect world God

created. We live in a fallen world, a world marked by man's sin. God's design, though still visible, is distorted and marred. Both man and nature show the effects of sin. Man hides from God. Weeds grow. Marriage is fraught with pain as well as pleasure. And singleness flourishes.

There was no singleness in Eden. Of newly-created man God said, "It is not good that the man should be alone; I will make him a helper fit for him" (Genesis 2:18). When God brought Eve to Adam, he recognized her as an integral part of himself, yet somehow "other"; as "bone of my bones and flesh of my flesh," (Genesis 2:23) yet different. "At last," we are told (verse 23), "at last" man's quest for something to satisfy his need was ended. And that evening, when God looked over his handiwork, he did not merely pronounce it "good" as he had on the five previous occasions, but "very good" (Genesis 1:31).

So singleness is one of the results of sin in the world — one of a host of evils in which we all share. It is hardly fair to blame it on God. He never intended that it should exist, any more than that there should be war, famine, sickness, pain, disease, or death. Man destroyed the perfection of God's creation so that now we live in only a hollow shell of what he intended for us; so man must suffer the consequences.

And suffer he does, in a thousand ways. And since nowhere is the image of God more deeply stamped upon man's being than in his sexual nature, nowhere is the effect of sin seen and felt more devastatingly than there.

Even more so is this true of woman. Through her body the promised Redeemer was to come, and with her the battle was joined in an especially intimate way. What more certain, then, but that in her sexual nature she should know intense sorrow and pain, as well as ecstasy? Both men and women suffer in their sexual natures because of sin; and one of the ways such suffering comes is in the anomaly of being single.

Strange, isn't it, how we are able to recognize that although natural disaster is the result of sin's presence in the world, it is not necessarily, if ever, connected with the sin of the people who experience it? Yet we tend to feel that a personal sorrow, such as being single, may well be due to personal weakness or inadequacy, or be otherwise deserved in some way by the person who bears it.

Jesus gave clear teaching on this subject. Concerning the man born blind (John 9), when the disciples asked whose sin had caused the blindness, he emphatically stated that neither the sin of the blind man nor of his parents had anything to do with it — he was blind in order that God's works might be made manifest through him. He stated the same truth concerning Lazarus' illness — it was for the glory of God (John 11:4). Then with two mighty miracles he demonstrated that glory before a wondering world.

The Christian church might well take note of this teaching. Why is it that there is great sympathy and succour for the Christian who suffers from one kind of disaster — accident, bereavement — and a total lack of understanding and concern for one who suffers from another — that of being single — which may well prove to be the heavier burden in the long run? Christians would do well to ponder this. We should realize that we must not make general statements about the single state; people may be single for a variety of reasons. And though any number of intimate personal griefs might be substituted here for being single, there is a principle here that should be investigated honestly before God. Far from being helped by their fellow Christians, all too many suffering people know only one silent sorrow added to another because of ignorance and wrong attitudes on the part of others. Single people should not have to be targets for tactless personal questions, unwelcome teasing and crude, embarrassing "jokes".

If this has been an aside, it is an important one. But back to being single as a result of sin.

Does this mean that single people cannot hope to experience God's best in their lives? Not for a moment. Our God is a God of redeeming grace. He meets us where we are, all of us suffering under the curse of sin in one way or another. He redeems married people from the many-faceted effects that sin has marked upon marriage. He redeems single people from the loneliness and incompleteness that is inherent in being single. Touched by God's grace, being single becomes a good thing — even God's best — for those who choose to seek it in him.

As a result, many have found in the single state an avenue of devotion and service towards God and man. God has used them significantly in the work of his kingdom. And so rich and widespread is his common grace that even those who do not recognize it or acknowledge him as Lord are enriched by it. Some opt for being single as their chosen way of life.

The good news of the gospel is that Jesus Christ has triumphed over sin, and we, if we will, may triumph with him. His victory does not remove the results of man's fall — sin is still with us, and the sorrows that follow in its wake. The single state still exists, and will continue to be an undesired way of life for many.

But its power is broken. No one need endure it in the bitterness of soul that Satan intended when he invented it. Jesus Christ is Lord. The Christian may know Christ's lordship in the strange, difficult matter of his being single.

Why are there single people? That the works of God might be made manifest in the deepest recesses of our beings. To declare God's glory in a fallen world. To show that God is enough for the human heart. To demonstrate to earth and hell and heaven the triumph of the life of God in the soul of man.

3
Sexuality

I must have been in my mid-twenties before I began to distinguish clearly between the sensuality of sex and sexuality itself. It was the beginning of a long pilgrimage.

I had begun teaching in 1935 at the age of 20. It was at the heart of the Depression. The only job I could find was in a lonely outpost in the Canadian Shield in the far north of Ontario, many hundreds of miles from home. There, as it turned out, I was to spend seven long, lonely years, first in a lumber camp, then in a gold-mining community. During the last three of these years, World War II was raging.

Adjusting from home life in the heart of Toronto to life in the backwoods was a difficult experience, to say the least. I thought I had stepped on to Mars, and I'm sure the poor folk among whom I worked thought I must have come from there. I was unutterably lonely. Culturally and socially, I found no fellowship. I did not understand the people, and they did not understand me.

Worst of all, I had no Christian teaching or companionship during those years. I had grown up in the heart of a large evangelical church. As a student I had been a group leader in the work of Inter-Varsity Christian Fellowship, then in its infancy in North America. Here all my friendships and activities were centred. Now I stood absolutely alone. This was a hard situation for any young person to face. It threw me on to the horns of a very personal dilemma. As a Christian, I knew I could not marry an unbeliever; and who else was there? I was forced to take a long, hard look at my circumstances, and to conclude that I might never marry. Whether for the present or for always I did not know, but I began to reflect seriously on the implications of being single.

As a Christian, I believed that marriage was God's gift to give or to withhold. He never promised it to anyone. It was not my inalienable right. I had come from a broken home, and I knew that there were worse things than being single. I realized I was glad that the choice was God's.

Years before, I had committed the whole matter of marriage to God and asked him to work out his plan for me. It was a bit hard to watch the years slipping by with no sign that he was doing anything about that commitment, while one by one my friends were marrying and I was constantly faced with the relentless inquiry, "When are *you* going to get married?" —this from Christians who should have known something about commitment, not to mention tact. But I trusted God, though not without occasional qualms. The matter was in his hands. Basically, I was willing to leave it there. There seemed little I could do about it in any case.

Somehow, neither then nor in the years that followed did I feel that I should make marriage a particular subject for prayer. What is commitment, anyway? God had promised to perfect what concerned me, and to keep what I had committed to him. Now and again, at some point of crisis, I would renew my commitment and reaffirm my trust in God's faithfulness. But my prayers have been that I might be kept in all the will of God, sensitive and obedient to his leading, and interceding for the things of his kingdom. I have never regretted this viewpoint, although I have not married. God's will is the one place in which I can't go wrong, whether about marriage or anything else.

Faced with being single, then, whether temporarily or permanently, I pondered deeply about many things. As a Christian single, I knew that I could not have sexual relations — sex was out. The Scriptures clearly forbade fornication, adultery and all homosexual practices. I accepted these restrictions as part of the cost of discipleship, though not without some deep, wordless struggles. But certain other things puzzled me.

The word sexuality was unknown to me then, but I had begun to discover something of its meaning. God had given me a friendship with a vibrant, creative woman about twelve years my senior. She was the wife of a minister in another community. She had opened her heart and her home to me, and we enjoyed a profound friendship from the time I was 18 until her death twenty years later. From her I caught a glimpse of some of the joy and wonder of being a woman, and a whole new world began to open up before me. My question: if I didn't marry, would I have to forgo all enjoyment of what I later learned to call my sexuality, which at that time seemed to be identified only with marriage?

I doubt if that rare woman ever dreamed how much she taught me of things pertaining to life and godliness! At the time I had no language to discuss such matters (if anyone of my generation did, I never met them). Books on such matters were virtually non-existent — how much better things are today! So we did not talk of these things overtly, and it was years before I could articulate what I learned; but I learned.

She was the epitome of Christian womanhood. From her, though all unknown to her, I absorbed, as by osmosis, the true meaning of womanhood. I observed that true womanhood requires true maturity, which is not easy for anyone to attain. I realized that it is more important in this life to be a whole person, God's true woman, than to be a married woman. I came to see that maturity is a personal and an individual thing, and that marriage in itself is no guarantee of maturity. Many a wife may be far from being a whole woman, with disastrous results to herself, her marriage and her family; many a single woman may be perfectly whole of spirit, a tower of grace and strength to all who know her.

I learned an infinity of practical things, too: how to manage and care for a home, how to cook, sew, decorate, garden, entertain and otherwise take delight in creative homemaking. I learned that housekeeping, even though difficult and demanding, if gladly and intelligently carried out need not be seen as drudgery, but may become a source of dignity and satisfaction. I saw how richly a home could be used in Christian nurture and witness. I began to find intense joy in such things, although until I was 40 home for me consisted of a drably-furnished bedsitter in the city centre. As I grew in the discovery of my womanhood, my horizons and my personality expanded. And gradually I came to realize that the expression of sexuality for a woman lay not only in the home, but in *all* forms of creative activity; and I began branching out in many directions.

Eventually, during those years and the ones that followed, I came to learn what I was unable to articulate until many years later — that God may place limits on our sexual behaviour, but never on the expression of our sexuality.

Human sexuality is not something apart from ourselves; it is what we are, our very essence. It is expressed in everything we do. It is the source of most of life's richest joys and fulfilments. God does not deny any of us the enjoyment or development of our sexuality. Christian single people are denied only the genital expression of sexuality; in all other ways we are free to express it to the utmost. And that "utmost" has a very broad scope.

Not that such denial is a small thing. But it is possible, and with God's help, it need not be devastating. It can even be enriching. One thing it is guaranteed to do for us if we are Christians: it will keep us clinging personally and purposefully to God for the rest of our lives. Who are we to dare to refuse a gift like that?

The enjoyment of sexuality, in ourselves and in others, is one of God's loveliest gifts. Those who for Jesus' sake have freely relinquished all right to the pleasures of its physical expression will not find themselves lacking in glad, life-affirming enjoyment of sexuality. In spite of this fact — maybe even because of it — they may develop a depth and richness of character, a self-fulfilling experience of life, a quality of self-giving service, a totality of being, as great as or even greater than if they had married.

Such fruition, of course, is not automatic. It springs from our total response to God, which consists of thousands of smaller responses, including our responses to our being single. We all know Christian single people of whom such fruition is true, and others of whom it is not. Which we are depends on what we do with what we have, and on our personal relationship with God.

4
The Sovereignty of God

What should I have done if I had not learned to rest upon the sovereignty of God? To know God, to know beyond the shadow of a doubt that he is sovereign and that my life is in his care — this is the unshakeable foundation on which I stay my soul. Such knowledge has deep significance for the single Christian.

What is wrong with me that life and love seem to have passed me by? What single person has not anguished over that question in the private depths of his heart? For somehow being single carries with it a stigma even today. One encounters unspoken — or spoken! — assumptions of inadequacy, of failure; one experiences a sense of shame at having been bypassed for no apparent reason. While a few people do remain single by choice, most of us find ourselves single against our deepest desires; and none of us is totally free from the sting.

Our culture reinforces such feelings in a thousand ways. Our whole society is couple-oriented. Parents expect their children to marry; so do their friends and relatives, and society at large. There are sexual tensions and strong peer pressures. Despite today's changing attitudes towards marriage, the person who marries late or not at all is considered an oddity, not quite normal. Sexual aberrations may be suspected, even hinted at. People feel free to question, to tease, to make sick jokes about being single as they would dare to do about no other personal matter. The world pairs off and the single person is left out of its activities. She no longer fits in at all; he, though he may still be welcome, soon finds he no longer really belongs. Though things are easier for single people today than ever before, there isn't a single person alive who has not suffered under some of these pressures. The single woman may have to live with the shattering knowledge that no one has ever desired her; the single man with the bitter fact that he has been rejected.

Eventually many of us come to believe that we must be some sort of misfit or we would have married. We struggle increasingly for a sense of identity and self-esteem. There may be certain elements of truth in some of these things, of course, though no more for single people than for couples. Married or single, none of us is fully mature. But for the Christian, basically the truth will lie in another direction altogether — in the mystery of the sovereignty of God. If we spent more time seeking our identity there and less in regret and self-deprecation and searching for partners, we would be better Christians and happier, more truly integrated people.

I shall always be thankful for an early knowledge of the sovereignty of God. I think I was always aware of this great truth, though it was many years before I learned to embrace it for myself and to live by its strength. It has sweetened the waters of singleness for me more truly than

I can tell, and lifted the burden of the stigma.

When I qualified as a teacher, I was unable to find work in my home city. It had never occurred to me that I might have to go far away to teach, let alone spend two years in a lumber camp and five in a mining camp to get started. I found the experience devastating. I accepted it because it was an economic impossibility to do anything else; but I was not resting in the sovereignty of God. I went north because I had to.

I knew that God was with me and would keep me, but I failed to see the situation as part of his plan. I can still remember the awful feeling I had that something must have gone wrong somewhere, that somehow I had got off course. I trusted God to bring me back — to my own preconceived notion of where I should be, no less! — rather than to choose for me and lead me in the right way. It all seems very childish to me now, of course, and it was. But I was barely 20 at the time, and no one had ever confronted me with the implications of God's sovereignty in down-to-earth everyday living. I knew it in theory only. I could wish I had been taught in a more truly scriptural way. But at least I was aware of it; and in sending me north the Holy Spirit began to make it real in my life.

Those were difficult years, lonely, turbulent, lacking in Christian teaching and fellowship. Yet even before they were over I was beginning to see in them some glimmerings of God's design. Eventually, much later, I came to know God's reason for those years, and I shall never be able to thank him enough for them.

Gradually, a step at a time, I was enabled to give up my non-existent "right to choose" and commit myself more and more completely to his sovereignty. Many things have been difficult for me to accept since then, but none has had quite the same power to shake me as that early experience did. The longer I know God the stronger is my confidence in his sovereign wisdom and love, and my certainty that my times are in his hands. I live with the unshakeable realization that there is nothing that can touch me, good or bad, that is not under the sovereign control of God. And this applies to my being single, as well as to everything else.

It was during those years in the north, 1935-42, the last years of the Depression and the first four years of World War II, that I found myself faced with the possibility of being single. I was still only grasping after the rest of faith that comes with the acceptance of God's sovereignty, and I knew much emotional turmoil and mental and spiritual anguish. None of it was spoken to any human soul. I was hundreds of miles away from anyone to whom I might have talked, and I had very little utterance for voicing my inmost thoughts in any case. It was a bleak and lonely experience. But slowly I began to note an inner difference. Was it really a little easier to trust God in this matter than in the crisis of my first job? Or was I perhaps coming to know God a little more truly for what he is? At any rate, the matter shone crystal clear. There was no way I could marry a non-Christian. Situated as I was at the time, my only alternative was to learn to live with being single.

The fact that an irrevocable decision had been reached did not mean that the battle was over; it had merely been joined. The basic issue was settled, but a thousand tensions remained, and choices had to be made again and again. The compass needle of mind and will might pull towards true north, but desires and emotions swung wildly to east or west from time to time. I can still remember how I felt when, having turned down for the third time an attractive date that I did not feel I could accept, I introduced the man to someone else, suggesting that he take her instead. He did, and married her within the year.

My notebooks from those years hold many entries in verse, few of them of any consequence. But two, perhaps, are pertinent here. Both were written the year I was 22. One of them is my initial witness to a commitment that is as real today as it was when it was first spoken.

> O hold my heart, Lord Jesus,
> Within thy wounded hand;
> Its stirring or its stilling
> Must come at thy command.
> My love is thine, my Saviour;
> No other sway I own;
> Bestow it where thou willest,
> Or keep it thine alone.

The second one is the poem *So Send I You,* which later became known as a song to John Peterson's setting and is found in many hymn books today. These words are somewhat lacking in true discernment of the Scriptures, for I had not yet learned that God's call is never to unmitigated gloom but is shot through with glory. Nonetheless they reflect something of the depth of commitment which was growing with my increasing knowledge of the sovereignty of God.

In those days I clung to God's sovereignty dumbly, desperately, as a drowning person clings to anything that will keep him afloat, no matter how unpleasant. Though I wouldn't have admitted it even to myself, in my heart of hearts I felt that this was a hard doctrine, demanding much — everything! — in return for what it gave. I suffered from the limited vision of youth, my own desires looming large and near and God's satisfactions seeming small and far away. I had not yet learned to rejoice in God.

Some years later I wrote a companion piece called *So Send I You* to go with that early poem. It shows the glory of the Christian commitment as well as its cost. I quote this truer version here (by permission of Singspiration Inc.):

So send I you — as I by God the Father
  Was sent to earth to give myself for man,
To spoil his foe, to wrest from death dominion,
  So send I you — to share th'eternal plan.

So send I you — by grace made strong to triumph
  O'er hosts of hell, o'er darkness, death and sin;
My name to bear, and in that name to conquer,
  So send I you — my victory to win.

So send I you — to take to souls in bondage
  The word of truth that sets the captive free;
To break the bonds of sin, to loose death's fetters,
  So send I you — to bring the lost to me.

So send I you — my strength to know in weakness,
  My joy in grief, my perfect peace in pain;
To prove my power, my grace, my promised presence,
  So send I you — eternal fruit to gain.

So send I you — in sorrow, yet rejoicing,
  As poor in store, yet boundless wealth to give;
As having naught, and yet possessing all things,

So send I you — the life of heaven to live.
So send I you — to bear my cross with patience,
And then one day with joy to lay it down;
To hear my voice, "Well done, my faithful servant;
Come, share my throne, my kingdom and my crown."
"So send I you .... "
"Lord, here am I, send me!"

How gracious God is; how gentle with his earth-bound children! Despite my reluctance to follow, little by little he led me deeper into his truth. How could I know that in committing myself to God's sovereignty I was embracing the richest love, the purest joys, the truest source of fulfilment the human heart can know?

5

"Why Aren't You Married?"

"Why aren't you married?" The question seldom comes to me now except from the lips of little children. Their innocent patter carries no sting. I respond easily in a variety of ways, suited to the questioner and the occasion.

It was not always so. In my twenties I found that query very hard to take. It is astonishing how many people assumed the freedom to ask it; every time I came down from the north I was bombarded by it. For the most part the questioners were Christians who should have known better. Apart from the rudeness of such an inquiry and the fact that it was none of their business, Christians should have displayed a greater sensitivity. More particularly, they should have known that the Holy Spirit works in each life according to his own design, not their stereotype, and should have been willing to allow him the time and room to do so. Yet not one of them thought to offer me support in the matter about which they interrogated me. Fortunately I had one or two friends who did.

Their queries covered me with confusion. I had always been inarticulate about anything that concerned me deeply. At that time I was struggling slowly and painfully towards a knowledge and acceptance of God's will in these areas of my life, and had trouble enough answering that question to myself, let alone to others. By the time I was sufficiently sure of my identity in Christ to be able to give a compelling answer, people were no longer questioning. Young people should not have to suffer from such lack of common courtesy and spiritual discernment on the part of older Christians.

The question, of course, is alive, often burning, in the heart of every single person. Sometimes it is well to take it out and look it in the eye.

There are many reasons why people do not marry even if they wish to, men and women alike. Some feel God calling them to single life in a religious order. Others opt for a single way of life for other reasons. Most single people past 35, looking back, can see valid factors that could have contributed to their being single. It is easy, though unproductive, to take refuge in them.

I think of my home background, which precluded normal social development; of the painful physical ailment which has plagued me from birth; of the narrow, legalistic atmosphere in which I passed my adolescence; of having to spend my years between 20 and 27 in isolation from other Christians; of returning to a more usual way of life only after three years of war had reduced the population of most Canadian cities to a predominantly female one, with three years of conflict yet to come. Any or all of these things are the human factors in my being single. Many, or most, single people can trace in their own lives some comparable chain of circumstances. And every

Christian woman must also face the fact that if she is to take her discipleship seriously, she greatly decreases her chances of marriage, for the Christian church has always been made up of more women than men.

But Christians who know God do not deal in human factors, nor recognize second causes. No *but's*, no *may-be's*, no *if only's* can haunt our dreams. God is the supreme reality in our life, and all that concerns us is under his control.

Romans 8 puts into words what a mighty cloud of witnesses have proved true in experience. Beside them I take my place. God is sovereign in the history of the universe and in the personal history of each of his children. He is working out his eternal plan, in which each Christian has his place. Sin, death and hell oppose on every side. Evil is strong, and sometimes it seems to have the victory.

Yet all the while, behind the scenes, God is sovereign. The victory of Calvary has not been and never will be abrogated. Nothing can touch my life but what God in love and wisdom permits. Why he allows what he does I do not know; but in everything that happens in my life he is working for my good and his glory. He never promised that that good would be visible now, though often parts of it are; it is my eternal good and usefulness and place in his purpose for which he is shaping me.

But God makes no mistakes. The ultimate triumph is his, and I am in his care.

This is the glory of the sovereignty of God, and it enfolds my single state, and yours. Within the shining sweep of its embrace there is no place for feelings of inadequacy or failure, of having missed the boat or been passed by. God has done it; it is enough.

In this assurance I can stand as tall as any married

woman or anyone else; move confidently among my kind free from the shackles of any stigma or reproach. I need not struggle for self-esteem. Without thinking of myself more highly than I ought, I know my worth to God and I accept the value he has placed on my life. My energies are not dissipated by envy or regret, but are focused on the work God gives me to do, and on worship and praise. I am free to live creatively and adventurously in union and fellowship with him. I accept my single state from God's hand, and rejoice.

A far cry from the long-ago years when "Why aren't you married?" could shake me for days! One grows slowly and painfully from timorous acceptance to praise and rejoicing, and there are many stumblings and heartaches on the way. Human desire never really dies — would we truly want it to? But its sting is drawn. It can be overwhelmed by the love and companionship of Jesus Christ. The important thing is to make the initial commitment, no matter how fearfully, and stick to it. God will do the rest.

6
Free To Be

Anyone who has had the temerity to stand up and affirm that God is greater than the problem of human singleness is certain to be the target of a thousand questions. Such has been my experience. I might say that I am better acquainted with the questions than with the answers.

However, most of the questions have been my own at one time or another — problems I have had to work through for myself alone with God. Some of them we shall consider now and in the following chapters. I do not pretend to know all the answers; I can only pass on what God has taught me, hoping that his Spirit may suit it to the needs of others and use it to help some struggling single person.

I have already touched on the question of identity. Who am I? This is something that all Christians, men and women, married and single, must settle early if they are to make progress in their Christian pilgrimage. Yet it is surprising how many single people at any age have never really faced it; and the same is true of married folk, particulary women. Indeed, the married woman may be much less likely to have sought her personal identity before God than her single sister; she may depend on her husband or family for her identity without ever knowing it, and simply bypass the whole issue. Witness the devastation and utter inability to cope with life that often attends widowhood.

I take my identity from Jesus Christ, not from any human relationship. The word of God tells me that I am complete in him (Colossians 1:10). While other relationships may give secondary identities — often very beautiful ones, as lover, husband, wife, parent, child, friend — the highest and truest identity, that of Christian, is open to all. I think of myself not as single, but as a *person*: first a Christian, then a woman, and finally a single woman.

My identity is eternal and unchanging. I am a child of God, of infinite worth to him. I am loved, chosen, called and united to him in the indissoluble bonds of his everlasting love. I have other identities as well — teacher, writer, homemaker, comrade, friend — but even if wife and mother were added to the list they could only modify my basic identity as a Christian, not change it. To have such assurance of identity is an infinite source of strength to any human being; and it is something that no one need be without. It is the initial step on the pathway to freedom and rejoicing for the single person.

Within the limits of Christian behaviour, good taste and thoughtfulness of others, I am free to be myself. I have no need to conform to others' ideas of what I should be. In whatever capacity I am functioning at a given time, I must strive for excellence — I should be a good teacher, a careful and creative writer, a trustworthy friend; but within these and scriptural boundaries, I know an immense freedom.

I can remember coming into the vestibule at church one icy-cold Sunday morning wearing a wool trouser suit under my fur coat. When a group of shivering, traditionally-dressed friends asked how I was, I responded blithely, "Thanking the Lord that I can wear boots and trousers to church on a bitter morning, instead of dress shoes and tights!" There was a ripple of rueful laughter in reply. Finally one of the girls spoke. "You mean if your name is Margaret Clarkson you can," she replied. "The rest of us can't." What she really meant was that such things were not really "done" at morning service at our church at that time; and while the others longed to do what I was doing, they did not have the inner freedom to do it. Those who find their identity in Jesus Christ find that he is easy to live with, as A. W. Tozer has said; and that on matters of personal freedom he is a most reasonable and human companion.

The freedom Christ gives grows as we grow in him. Ten years ago — even five years ago — I could not have written this book. My attitude to being single was the same then as it is now, but I did not have the inner freedom to speak such personal thoughts. Even now it takes all my courage to do so; but my freedom has grown until it is now possible. My thanks to the friends, editors and publishers who have encouraged me as I write!

A thoughtful new Christian made a penetrating observation to me a year or so after her conversion. An academic, she had been a stranger to any Christian community until she found Christ at the age of 46. Things that most of us take for granted were entirely new to her. She observed the Christian family from a different viewpoint than the rest of us, and every so often would come out with a remark that showed an insight far beyond that of many experienced Christians.

"I have come to the conclusion," she commented to me one day, apropos of nothing in particular, "that self-consciousness is the ultimate sin."

I thought about it for a time, and then agreed with her. True conversion should lead to a divinely-integrated self. Christians who have found their identity in God and accepted his freedom will no longer be self-conscious. Self-consciousness is the opposite of God-consciousness. The one inhibits personal freedom; the other bestows it. A Christian's consciousness will be focused upon God. Anything else is sin.

Sometimes our freedom may be put to the test. I attended Urbana '76 (American Inter-Varsity's missions conference for students) as the writer of the words of the theme hymn for that year. For unknown reasons I lay awake all the night before the closing day of the convention, being still awake at some time after 6 a.m. Then I must have dozed, for I woke suddenly to the sharp sound of the telephone. My bus would leave for the morning session in twenty minutes. I leaped into my clothes, pulling on a loose pullover rather than taking time to button my blouse, skipped jewelry and make-up, and bypassed washing my face and cleaning my teeth in favor of a quick cup of coffee. I completely forgot the tailored jacket that turned my trousers into a trim trouser suit, grabbed my coat and fled to the bus.

I arrived at the arena just in time to hear my name being called on the P.A. system: Would I please come to the platform? I was so shaken that I went without Bible or handbag. Reaching down for a tissue — I'm a great morning sneezer — I was thunderstruck to discover that I not only had no pocket, but no jacket either. There I stood in front of over 17,000 people, dressed in trousers and a sloppy jumper, faced with a microphone and the request to speak an unexpected word to the students.

Well, I gave a greeting and a brief word, concluding with two stanzas of a favourite hymn. As I heard the speakers assembling on the platform behind me, I stepped back from the mike and started to make for my place, my tissue and blessed anonymity. But a pair of strong arms grasped my shoulders from behind and steered me to a seat. "David Howard wishes you to remain on the platform", an authoritative voice murmured in my ear.

So there I sat for the next two and a half hours in front of the biggest crowd I ever expect to face, looking and feeling like a witch. Somehow a message had failed to reach me, and I had been caught totally unprepared. It did not help to discover, as I soon did, that Billy Graham and John Stott were among the group of notables sitting on the platform beside me.

It would have been easy to be utterly crushed by such an experience. Normally I appear properly groomed and dressed for an occasion. Any woman likes to look her best, and a sleepless night is poor preparation for a public appearance, let alone before 17,000! If I had to appear a fool, need it have been such a big fool?

But what did it matter? Who was looking at me anyway? Whom was I trying to impress? I rejoice to have been part of that magnificent convention, and to have been privileged to give a word of witness to my Saviour. I thank God for a sense of humour, and for Christian freedom. If I believe in the sovereignty of God, I must believe that he had something to do with that morning's happenings. There is no room for self-consciousness if God is all in all.

I have never felt the need to marry just so I wouldn't be single. Realizing that marriage was something that God might or might not give, I early set myself to embrace life fully, not merely to mark time. Above all, I have sought to know God; not just to know about him but to know him personally. He alone can give the freedom I need.

I've wanted to be a whole person, God's true woman; married or single is beside the point. I've wanted to cultivate all aspects of my personality as fully as possible, and that includes my sexuality. I've actively sought to cultivate certain things: the ability to make and sustain deep friendships with persons of all ages and both sexes; to be trustworthy, responsible, punctual; to work well with others — which, being something of an individualist, is something I do not find easy. I enjoy a lively sense of humour and a full and varied spectrum of interests, which increases with the years. I strive to reach my highest capacities mentally, creatively and professionally, and, of course, spiritually. I pray for, and seek to practise, a spirit of true thankfulness.

I fall far short of all these things. But such goals will enrich any life, married or single; and in so far as I have been able to attain to them, have greatly enriched mine. And they have stood me in particularly good stead, and added to my freedom, as a single woman.

7

Cheated?

"But have you never felt cheated?" The question comes frequently. The feeling of being cheated seems to be a common one among the never married. After all, we live only once; and we are expressly told that marriage is for this life only, having no place in heaven. It is not hard to see why those who have not had opportunity to experience marriage and parenthood might feel cheated.

At one stage in my life this question used to haunt me. I understand its torments very well. Holding someone else's child in your arms does something to you deep down inside.

But no, I do not feel cheated, and have not now for many a long year. Release comes with an increasing experience of God, whose nature is such that he could never cheat anyone, as those who truly seek him will surely find. This discovery can be reinforced by a liberal use of that well-known but rare commodity known as common sense, which most of us possess but all too frequently seem loath to use. If there is one weapon that single people should learn to use, it is this. Common sense is a great piece of armour with which to face life's battles.

God never promised anyone a husband, a home and three chubby children — nor health, happiness and prosperity either. Far more New Testament promises have to do with suffering than with material good or human well-being. God is doing something for eternity, not merely for time. The single state, as we have already seen, is one result of man's fall. All mankind must partake of the evils attendant upon man's sin, and in so doing, some of us are bound to remain single.

If my part of humanity's travail includes being single, how can I feel cheated? On sober reflection, which of life's other calamities would I prefer — blindness, deafness, mental retardation, insanity, quadriplegia, devastation by war, famine, natural disaster — to mention but a few? These are questions for serious consideration. Thousands of people do experience these things. But for the grace of God, so might we. Is being single that much worse?

Have you ever spent helpless months in hospital, in traction, perhaps, or on a Stryker frame? Have you ever visited a home for the handicapped or the chronically incapacitated, a hospital for sick children or for the mentally ill? Have you ever contemplated the lives of men and women who were crippled or paralyzed in infancy, maybe even before birth? Have you compared the desolation they must know with your own burden of being single — a burden many of them are forced to carry as an "extra" along with their physical disability? Then surely you can never again feel cheated.

When unworthy thoughts of being cheated plague you,

when you experience surges of desire or periods of depression, try counting your blessings before the Lord, literally and deliberately. Do as the song says and "name them one by one". Not only will it surprise you what the Lord has done, but before long you will be lost in shame and then in awe and worship, overwhelmed by God's goodness and mercy to you. Your being single simply won't matter any more. You will forget your feelings of being cheated.

A small brush with other troubles will show singleness in its true light. Personal experience makes this real to me. I've had a health problem all my life. Pain works devastation in every area of human life and personality, hedging me in in a thousand ways. It has held me back from doing many of the things that I have most wanted to do in life; and it is progressive. I find this situation infinitely harder to accept than being single. To be single with normal health would seem to me to be almost no problem at all.

Yet I have not been cheated. To feel cheated implies that I have been deprived of something that is mine by right. As a Christian, I have no rights — to marriage, to physical well-being, to anything but what God sends. The Christian knows only God's gifts. Perhaps those he has given me have thrown me more fully on his sufficiency than any other gifts he could have given me — who can tell? In any case, I know him increasingly as *El Shaddai* — the God Who Is Enough. And so may you.

Christian scholars have meditated much on Jesus' teachings about marriage and the resurrection. Obviously marriage as we know it will be unnecessary when there is no death and hence no need for the perpetuation of the race. I think it will more likely be superseded than abolished. It is not in the nature of God to deny his people any good thing; certainly not in the new creation when sin and darkness are past. It is reasonable to assume that the finest qualities in human relationships will be preserved, transfigured into something infinitely lovelier than anything we can know or can imagine now. What form this will take we cannot tell; but here is Dr Corbin Carnell's reflection on the matter ("Open and Closed Friendships", *Eternity* April 1977).

> When our Lord Christ said that in heaven there would be neither marrying nor giving in marriage, I don't think he was setting aside human sexuality. I hope that all the good things of earth will be incorporated in the new creation. Perhaps what he was saying in that passage is that in heaven we will not need to discipline the directing of our love so carefully. We will then be in the presence of the Father who gives the Son, and the Son who gives the Holy Spirit, and the Spirit who glorifies the Son, and the Son who obeys the Father. We, too, will then be able to participate in a great mutuality of loves.

And if that is not true, the truth is something even better!

8
Loneliness

The question of loneliness is a common one, and one for which there is no easy answer. I think it is safe to say that in general, most single people will experience more loneliness than most married folk. As far as I can see, single people must just make up their minds to accept this reality and then seek ways of combating it. No solution is going to drop down out of the blue; we must find, or make, our own answers to this question.

I remember visiting in the home of a friend one evening when there was a knock at the door. My friend introduced the newcomer as Principal of the college where he was a professor, which was part of a large university. The guest apologized for dropping in uninvited.

"This is my wife's study group night," he explained, "and both the girls had to go out. That left me the only one at home. You know what a helpless creature a man is when he's all alone in a house!" he said, turning to his colleague with a forlorn little gesture. Then, with half-shamed laughter, he concluded, "I knew you'd take me in."

The words fell strangely on my ears. A man of godliness and of letters, a leader among Christian men, unable to face the prospect of one evening alone in his own home! I had been alone then for well over twenty-five years, and had no prospect of ever living any other way. Yet I did not really find it a burden. I knew the companionship of Jesus Christ.

So did he, of course, as well as the couple in whose home we met. My Christian commitment was no greater than theirs. But my need was — and that was the crux of the matter. I knew the companionship of Christ in the intimacy of my home life because I had no other companionship there.

This is what Samuel Rutherford meant when he wrote, "Our needs best qualify us for Christ." My loneliness had driven me to seek and to cultivate Christ's companionship. My married friends had no such gnawing need except in a general way. Without even realizing it, they depended on one another for fellowship. When that was lacking, they felt lost. I, never having known such companionship, constantly turned to God for a fellowship which enabled me to be happily alone anywhere.

It has never ceased to amaze me that the married women in the summer cottages round about mine at the River, while proclaiming loudly that they wish they could stay there during the week as I do, invariably return with their husbands to the city on Sunday nights. There could be good reasons for this and probably are. But the wives, whom I've known well for years, tell me that the real reason is that they can't bring themselves to stay alone. Some admit to feeling fear, others do not; but by their own admission, they all feel incapable of handling their loneliness. I have cheerfully stayed alone at my cottage through

July and August for thirty-six years, and now my summers stretch to include the uninhabited months of June and September as well — and I thoroughly enjoy it. I don't know of any place where I feel less lonely than at the cottage. I am much more likely to experience spells of loneliness when in densely-populated Toronto.

I've never been quite able to account for this, except to suspect that summer sunshine, warm waters and the freedom to indulge my love of nature in all the shy, wild things round about has something to do with it. The city is vast, impersonal, noisy and exhausting, even though it does hold fine friendships and fascinating things to do. In any case, I can and do live happily alone in both places.

The companionship of Jesus Christ through the Holy Spirit is no myth. He is the first Person I speak to in the morning and the last at night. Many days he is the only One with whom I may talk all day. I try not to have too many days of such isolation, but sometimes they are inevitable. Their hours, however, are usually very happy.

We don't talk only of spiritual things, he and I, although that, of course, is part of each day's fellowship. We keep up a running conversation all day long, whatever I may be doing. I'm constantly needing his help with this problem, that undertaking, this attitude and that temptation, and it's always available. He helps with such practicalities as reminding me that I left the iron on, that I should run an errand or make a phone call, or by jogging my memory as to where I set something down — like my glasses!

Together we enjoy the beautiful things with which he has filled my life — fine music, restful colours and textures, the soft, sinewy feel of a furry body, the flashing jewel of a bird's wing, the rose and amber of an evening sky, the fragrance of dewy flowers, the friendliness of a crackling fire on an autumn night. Together we share many a good book, concert, play or ballet, and many a good joke. Together we create a song, a poem, an evening dress or a trouser suit, together plan and write an article or a book. My heart is constantly reaching up to him in gratitude and praise by day and often far into the night. In return, he fills it with himself.

Such a situation did not come about overnight. I have had my times of loneliness and dismay, many of them; and occasionally I still do. But in so far as I give myself to God in a glad and grateful sharing of life, he gives himself to me.

For to God's single people, singleness is his gift. Whereas marriage is called "honourable" by the writer to the Hebrews (Hebrews 13:4), and Paul states that those who marry have "not sinned," (1 Corinthians 7:28) both Jesus and Paul speak of being single as a gift (Matthew 19:22; 1 Corinthians 7:7). Paul also designates it as a good thing (1 Corinthians 7:8, 26, 28). And James teaches that all God's gifts are good, even perfect (James 1:7). Our human nature does not easily see singleness in this light, but such is the teaching of the word of God.

If God has given us the gift of being single, which is bound to include loneliness, then he has also given us the gifts that are needed to sustain it. These are not likely to burst upon us full blown; it is up to us to discover them and to learn to use them. Paul urges us not to neglect the gifts that are in us, but to stir them up and put them to work (1 Timothy 2:14; 2 Timothy 1:6).

God's gifts may not always follow our natural inclinations, but they will be there, and they will meet our needs. We may find them in unlikely places — an illness, perhaps, may force us to be alone long enough that we learn to cope with loneliness because we must, and ever afterwards are grateful for mobility and the privilege of moving about among others. Or casual attendance at a study centre may uncover a latent talent for music or writing, painting or photography, and we may spend long, solitary hours developing it, only to discover that we have found a friend whose companionship will nourish us in our aloneness for the rest of our lives. We may have to seek out our sustaining gifts, but we will find that we have the ones we need. God does not leave his single people to cope with being single on their own!

I don't know all the answers to human loneliness. But I do know the main one: a true acceptance of the total will of God, and the deliberate daily, hourly, even momentary practice of his presence. One learns it simply by doing it; there is no other way.

Single people must work out other practicalities of living, of course, each for himself. What works for one does not necessarily work for all. Suggestions given for problems discussed in other chapters of this book will prove useful in combating loneliness as well. But no solution that you or I can invent, nor all of them together, can deliver us from loneliness unless we have first learned to draw on the companionship of Christ. That is the basic answer to the question of how to live alone in serenity and peace.

9
Depression

Depression, like loneliness, is a part of life. We all suffer from it at one time or another. For unknown reasons, we wake up some mornings engulfed in inner gloom and hopelessness which may last for days. Dark and dismal mornings may provide fertile soil for such feelings, but they do not cause them — we also experience depression on sunny days. Nor are circumstances the cause. Trying times may make it harder to withstand depression, but we may also feel depressed when things are going well. We are human; that is the reason.

Depression may vary from vague feelings of unhappiness, restlessness and incompleteness, through an increasing sense of inner disunity, woe, uncertainty and inability to cope, to a swelling tide of all-encompassing darkness that may require professional help. Few of us escape it entirely.

Nor is depression peculiar to single people. Married folk experience it just as much. In general, women suffer from depression more than men. Because single women must earn their own living and have had to learn to produce on the job regardless of how they feel, they sometimes cope with depression a little more easily than married women whose work is done at home.

Many factors can contribute to the degree of power that depression may exercise over us. Too much pressure, too little sleep, too many fast-fry meals eaten in too much of a hurry, not enough exercise — such things can make it hard to withstand an attack of depression. So can personal problems, especially unresolved ones, and any kind of spiritual distance or alienation from our Father. We must guard against anything that would lower our resistance physically, mentally and especially spiritually, and so allow an attack of depression to overwhelm us. For depression is one of Satan's tools to render God's people useless in his service. He is constantly on the lookout for any crack through which he may gain entrance to our beings and thus enmesh us from within in the black net of depression.

Depression must be fought with spiritual weapons, aided by common sense.

Common sense tells us that if we are depressed we should not spend time needlessly alone, but seek company. It tells us that a true confidant is worth his weight in gold; that a burden shared is only half a burden. It tells us that hard work is an excellent antidote to depression, for it is impossible to be totally absorbed in two things at once. It demonstrates that physical activity will release tension. It teaches that personal pain may be transmuted into some form of creative service that will bless not only the creator but others as well. It affirms that today's darkness will not last for ever, and resolutely goes ahead with each day's demands as if depression did not exist.

Faith goes even further. Faith believes that God is present in the darkness, even though she is unable to realize his presence; she knows him as "the light that shone in the darkness, and the darkness could not put it out." Faith not only calls on God for power to destroy the works of the prince of darkness, but for grace to reap spiritual harvest from his attack. Faith knows that at times when prayer seems unable to penetrate the thick clouds that hide God's presence, praise will invariably clear a pathway to his throne.

I am no stranger to depression. I have had more than enough experience in seeking to escape its unwelcome embrace. I know that there is no one way of deliverance, though there are many things that will help.

Perhaps the single greatest weapon is praise. There is nothing that a person in the grip of a severe depression wants to do less than to praise. Nonetheless it is praise that opens the dungeon door and sets the prisoner free. An unknown writer tells why:

> For praise is purer far
> Than any form of prayer;
> Prayer climbs the steep ascent to Heaven —
> Praise is already there.

Praise does not depend on how we feel, but on what God is. When we learn to rest on this truth and throw ourselves utterly upon God, we are well on the way to overcoming depression.

We must learn to praise God deliberately, out of the depths if necessary, but to praise in any case. In *Pilgrim's Progress* Bunyan tells us that when Christian was lodging at the Palace Beautiful and was discussing the difficulties of the way with his hosts, Prudence asked him:

"Can you remember by what means you find your annoyances, at times, as if they were vanquished?"

Christian replied:

"Yes, when I think what I saw at the cross, that will do it; also when I look upon my broidered coat, that will do it; also when I look into the roll that I carry in my bosom, that will do it; and when my thoughts wax warm about whither I am going, that will do it."

And so we look at God and at what he has done for us, and as we view one wonder after another, we, too, exclaim, "*That* will do it!"

We praise God for what he is — and the more we have contemplated his attributes and experienced him for ourselves when things are well with us, the more easily we shall be able to praise in the darkness of depression. We praise God for what he has done. We praise him for what he is doing now, whether we are sensible of his present working or not. We praise him for what he will do, both in time and in eternity, as if we possessed it now. We praise him for his promises and hold them fast, even though they may seem to our present mood to be utterly incapable of fulfilment. You will remember that it was when Christian and his companion secured the Key of Promise that they were freed from the power of Giant Despair and escaped from Doubting Castle. So it will be with us.

Fragments of scriptures learned in happier days will be used by the Holy Spirit to supply help in time of need. These may be of any length, but are often quite short — a sentence, a phrase, even one or two words. To combat the shattering sense of inner disunity and disharmony that is a part of depression, how often I have cried to God in the words of Psalm 86:11 — "Unite my heart to fear thy name!" — and known his healing touch! And I could not count the hours I have lived by the strength of the one word, "Jesus!" It's a good idea to jot down helpful texts as you encounter them and to keep them ready for use in times of need.

Lines from the great hymns of the church have seen me through many a dismal day. Their rhyme, rhythm and music make them easy to remember. In times of stress I cast about in my mind for something especially suitable, then set it turning on the invisible turntable of my mind and keep it playing sometimes for days. It may be a lofty thought encased in noble verse and set to sublime music, as the chorale "My Father, Let Thy Will Be Done" from Bach's *St. Matthew Passion*, which bore me through a rough time that followed a bad medical prognosis years ago. It may be one of today's fragrant "scripture songs", or something as unsophisticated and sweet as the simple song, "God is so good, he's so good to me", which have also seen me through more than one dark hour. Wise is the Christian who stores his heart and mind "in sunshine weather" with words that will nourish his soul in times of darkness!

10
Roots

How have you met the need for permanence? This is one of the easier questions I have been called on to answer.

Most people need a sense of permanence. There may be a few vagrant souls whose home is where they hang their hat, who itch for constantly changing scenes. But most of us need a sense of belonging, of putting down roots in a spot where our hearts can rest and calling it home. Heartsease is found in varying situations for varying people. Yours will not likely be the same as mine, but it will be as valid for your needs as my solutions have been for mine.

I first consciously put down roots when, aged 26, I bought an isolated, rundown summer cottage, whose only approach was — and still is — by water. Here I have spent my summers ever since, and here I am writing this book today.

The cottage gave me my first real opportunity to

develop my homemaking instincts. It is impossible to say what it has meant to me over the years. I bought it on such a financial shoestring that in order to make a go of it at all I had to adapt — to learn to create, invent and make do. I learned to handle and care for a boat, repair a dock, shingle a roof, knock out a wall, make or remodel furniture, cut my own wood and ice, make rugs, paint, design and anything else that needed doing. I found endless delight in all these varied challenges.

The cottage has proved to be an excellent place in which to repay hospitality shown me by my married friends, who, with their children, could not always be entertained when I lived in bedsitters. Here youngsters can spill out all over the rocks and woods and into the river, making excellent visits possible with a minimum of strain. Not that there isn't any: I recall one long-ago weekend when I had wall to wall beds laid out on the floor and no less than nine guests — and a three-day blow with a never-ceasing torrent of rain! But we had a good time none the less.

During my years here I have witnessed great changes in the community — in fact, a community has grown up around me. For a number of years now I have been the "original inhabitant" hereabouts, and something of a legend — especially to young folk who constantly ask me for tales of "life in the early days"! Everyone on this part of the river now has arrived much more recently than I. I belong here in a sense that no one else does.

I've watched nearly three generations grow up here, and many kinds of development taking place, not all of it welcome. Here I have lived close to earth and sky and water, have known God's creatures and studied his handiwork, have learned his secret wonders. I can still predict tomorrow's weather by the sky, and am more likely to be accurate than most of the forecasts heard on the radio.

Here I have done almost all my writing, learning to live happily quite alone for weeks at a time in order to give birth to a book. Here, too, friendships have been born and nourished. A very great sense of permanency and belonging has come to me because of my cottage. The roots of my heart are buried deep in the Pre-Cambrian rock of the Canadian Shield.

Not until I was 40 was I able to exchange a furnished room in Toronto for a home of my own, and words cannot express the blessing it has been to me. Seven years ago I moved from my first tiny bungalow where I had spent seventeen happy years, leaving the busy street for a quieter, more secluded setting on a suburban ravine where I look out on an incredible expanse of valley, wood and sky. God's lines have fallen unto me in pleasant places, indeed. I am very conscious of his presence in my home, and of his care of me.

Home ownership invites involvement — with neighbours, with schools, with community projects, with municipal affairs, carried on simultaneously in the two communities, city and country, where I am a rate payer. At the same time I taught school for thirty-eight years, the last thirty of them for one Board of Education (Toronto), and this brought involvement of another kind. I spent over forty years in one church, where I saw three generations of young people grow up and countless others come during their university years. All these things have given me a sense of purpose, of continuity, of permanence. I belong in a very real way. I think that I experience life more fully in one place than if I kept moving about, although this is not necessarily true for everyone. Besides, there's nothing like a good healthy mortgage to make a person put down roots!

Having a home has given me greater credibility with my

non-Christian neighbours and colleagues. I can trade yarns and household hints with the best of them; talk land values, equities, interest rates; share good workmen. I think it has given me a special sense of kinship with my married friends, too. In one way, at least, my life is identical to theirs — our houses have to be maintained, decisions made, repairs carried out, improvements planned and implemented. Gardens have also been a point of contact, as we shared lore of growing flowers, fruits and vegetables, as well as seeds, roots and produce.

These homemaking ventures have necessarily developed in me a sense of responsibility. With only my own ingenuity to fall back on, I have had to face the same situations that householders everywhere must face — appliances that break down, woodworm in the loft, a broken water main causing the lawn to sink, a roof that leaks, gutters to be repaired or renewed, a house that must be painted. Most households have two partners, and I am alone. It is hard to supervise workmen when you must be teaching some miles away while they are paving your drive, putting your house on mains drainage or replacing the condenser in your freezer. It is possible to come home to find that they are paving your neighbour's drive instead of yours. It would be good to have someone else on whom to rest part of the burden.

But when I first discovered what was involved in managing the cottage by myself, I vowed two things: I would not be a woman who went whining for help, trying to make people feel sorry for her and so give her special attention; and I would not be a woman who begged help from the husbands of her friends and neighbours. If I can, I do my work myself — and it's astonishing what a woman with a mind to work can do. If I can't, I have it done by local workmen at the going rates and tell my friends about it afterwards. If I can't afford to do that, I wait until I can. But above all, I have learned to lay my burdens on the one shoulder strong enough to carry them. I find him a sensitive and capable companion.

"The government shall be upon his shoulder." I could tell tale after tale of how God has met my need in practical ways, but one must suffice.

Some years ago I needed a new roof on my cottage. Owing to severe spinal surgery, I could take no part in the work myself. I arranged with a slow-spoken carpenter some miles away to come and do the work when he could. I knew it might be the next summer before he got around to it, but I could afford to wait. I'd learned to plan with local customs in mind.

The next summer came and went with no word from the roofer. Before I could contact him the following July, I suffered a nasty fall on the rocks, injuring my spine so that I was unable to walk. I crawled to the boat and headed for the call box two miles distant. There I talked with my surgeon, who told me to lie motionless on a board for three days, then call him and make arrangements to come to Toronto if things worsened.

The cottage is still quite isolated, and I have no near neighbours. I knew I ought not to be alone. But that night things began to happen. The son of new cottagers whom I had not yet met had overheard my phone call and watched me crawl to the boat. His father arrived at my dock in short order, offering to drive me to the city, or to bring food and letters daily while I lay flat. Early next morning another boat arrived. It was my long-awaited roofer, who unloaded his materials.

His work lasted three days. All that time, without having to ask anyone to come, I had help when I needed it, and could send messages in and out. What made that carpenter come at that particular time? What but the gentle prompting of the faithful One upon whose heart and shoulder are all my affairs?

And here I must witness to God's faithfulness in the matter of providing help and in assisting me in my dealings with workmen. Every householder must find and employ workmen from time to time, and, if he is alone, trust them to carry out their work in his absence. I knew nothing more than any novice about such things, and to this day the sudden need to hire workmen fills my heart with an uneasy dismay. But in the nearly forty years that I have had the sole care of property as part of my life, I have never once suffered at the hands of a contractor, and only once or twice have I been even slightly disappointed in the work done — mostly I have been more than happy with it. This is due to no ability of my own; so God shepherds those who commit the planning and keeping of their affairs to him.

Seeking a sense of permanency in a home is hard work — hard both physically and emotionally. Especially at first there were times when it seemed almost impossible to carry on. I was under constant financial pressure. I never knew when I might come home to find that the boiler had burst and the house was haunted by the Ghost of the Furnace Past, or the septic tank had given up the struggle. These were problems with which I had had no experience, and with which I did not know how to cope. But having a home has also been for me a most blessed experience, an unspeakable joy and a splendid investment. The sense of venturing out entirely on my own with God as my partner has been exhilarating, intimate and precious, a magnificent way of coming to know God and of proving his sufficiency. I recommend such adventure to any single person desiring a home and a sense of permanency.

A home may not be everyone's cup of tea. Your solution may lie in an entirely different direction. Whatever it is, seek it with a sense of adventure and delight. With Christ as your companion, you are a creature of eternity. Why should you lack for a sense of permanency?

No true Christian should know such a lack, for God has promised to all his children the ultimate permanency — that of spiritual fruitfulness. Christ living in us, pouring himself out to others through us, is sure to yield spiritual fruit as others are born anew or nurtured in the things of God. The permanency of lands and houses is temporal, but that of fruit borne to Jesus Christ is eternal.

11
Fulfilment

How can I be fulfilled if I don't marry? The question is a common one, and not without reason. It is only natural to seek to fulfil oneself in marriage and parenthood. Our human sexuality cries out for such fulfilment, for fruition. Our hearts and minds long intensely for spiritual and physical closeness, for union with one we love, one whose love can complete us and enable us to fulfill our destiny as man or woman.

What is the Christian single person's answer to the need for fulfilment?

First we must think of what fulfilment really means. In today's frantic search for fulfilment we tend to think of the goal as self-fulfilment. True fulfilment, however, consists in something outside ourselves. For the Christian, it lies in fulfilling God's plan for his life and sharing in his eternal purposes. While physical fulfilment is a gracious gift of God, it is not the deepest source of satisfaction in life even for the non-Christian, and certainly not for the Christian.

It is a mistake to think of fulfilment primarily in terms of biology. A little sober thought will make us realize that some of the most unfulfilled persons on earth are those who have had many marriages — witness Hollywood! The examples of history and our own observation of life tell us that sexual experience is not essential to human fulfilment.

Was the Lord Jesus Christ an unfulfilled person? Yet he was single. We are told that he was tempted in all points just as we are, which means that he, too, must have been tempted to reach out for physical fulfilment. Yet he who had no home, no property, no family, who died as a common criminal nailed to a cross, knew no sin, but lived and died in the perfect fulfilment that comes of being one with God and doing his will. Almost his last words were that he had finished the work the Father had given him to do. To believe that Jesus Christ was unfulfilled, he who in his life and death fulfilled more than any other who has ever lived, is to believe a lie.

History abounds with proof that single men and women may be profoundly fulfilled without sexual experience. Most of those whose names stand out spent their lives in service towards others. Great humanitarians like Florence Nightingale and Tom Dooley; great missionaries like Mary Slessor and Amy Carmichael; great saints like Francis of Assisi and Fanny J. Crosby — even the man in the street who might not understand their motivation would recognize them as fulfilled persons. And we all know men and women, our own friends and neighbours, whose lives display the calm of quiet content, the settled joy of fulfilment, though denied fulfilment in the physical sense of the word.

Although single, I certainly do not feel that I am

unfulfilled. Rather, I marvel that God has allowed me to experience so many and varied satisfactions in life. Everyone knows areas of unfulfilment in this world. This is true even of those within the finest of Christian marriages — not to mention those to whom marriage has brought no fulfilment at all. So, in common with humankind, I am fulfilled, though not totally. My sexual fulfilment, among other things, is only partial — something I suspect I share with many, if not most, married people. But there are many other fulfilments in life besides the sexual, and I am rich in many of these.

A great many sources of fulfilment await discovery by God's single people, sources as rich and varied as are the needs that require them. And most of them are waiting close at hand.

Work stands high on the list. Blest indeed are those whose daily work brings with it true and deep satisfaction. Not everyone is so fortunate; but even if his work is routine and less than absorbing, the Christian may find fulfilment in it by doing it for Christ, while seeking at the same time to qualify for some more rewarding work for the future. If we seek fulfilment from our work, it must have some element of nobility inherent in it, and we must throw our whole hearts into its performance. Basically, we get as much out of our work as we put into it. Poor workmanship will never yield fulfilment to anyone.

Home may be one of the richest sources of personal fulfilment. I say "may be" because all too many single people seem to feel that lacking the presence of a marriage partner, home is merely a place to hang a hat and sleep. Those who invest time and thought and creativity in their home, however, whether it is a bedsitter, a flat or a house, will find fulfilment there.

Many single people feel that home is merely a temporary affair until a partner materializes, and so rob themselves by never putting down roots, never making an investment in such sources of satisfaction as fine music, fine works of art, a garden, an animal or other similar things. While no one's home should be an idol, it is a wise single person who invests as deeply in his home as he would if he or she were married. Home is something we all need, a gift of God that all single people should take seriously. It can also be a wonderful focus for Christian service of many kinds, and for practising the arts of friendship and hospitality.

Some single people enjoy a sharing of life by sharing living quarters with one or two friends; others find they do better alone. There are advantages both ways. Some hesitate to share for fear of being branded homosexual. Such accusations are sometimes made, even by Christians. Their best answer is silence. If your heart is transparent before God, and he does not check you, do as you please. If you find joy in sharing, then share, in Christian freedom. The choice is yours — make it, and then set about building yourself a home. Don't deny yourself the fulfilment it can hold for you!

What can give a deeper sense of fulfilment than a true friendship? Here single people may have an advantage over married folk, whose friendships are usually made in couples where the two men as well as the two women must mutually desire them — a more complicated arrangement than friendship on a one-to-one basis. We are free to make friends wherever we find them — and the single person who walks with God will not lack for true, abiding friendships. It is impossible for me to speak my immense gratitude to God for the beautiful friendships I have received at his hand. Apart from himself, I consider them my greatest wealth. Every encounter with a stranger is an exciting adventure, the possible start of a new and rewarding friendship. When I consider the astonishing ways God has of bringing his children together in friendship, how can I doubt that he could have done the same with a marriage partner had that been his plan for my life?

Friendship is an art that must be actively cultivated. It seldom, if ever, just happens. It is not enough to desire to have friends; we must be alert, outgoing towards others, willing to give friendship, not just to receive it. True friendship costs — in time, in energy, in involvement, in self-giving. To love a friend is to become vulnerable, to run the risk of being hurt, of suffering. No matter. There is nothing more truly worth having in this world than a God-given friendship.

Friendships should be with other single people, with couples, with both sexes, and with all ages, including children; with people who live near and with people who live far away. They should be with those we need, and with those who need us. Most of them will be with people we meet in the natural course of events as we walk with God, for God brings his own friends together in remarkable ways. He delights in a good friendship.

Friendships lead to shared activities — concerts, plays, holiday trips or other time spent together. Friends may study together, learn new skills and hobbies, share in creative activities, garden, ramble, watch birds, photograph, collect things together. Many such creative and re-creative activities may also be carried on alone; and it's a wise single person who learns to enjoy hobbies in solitude as well as with others. Solitary hours that would otherwise be lonely may be filled with happiness and usefulness because of them. And none of us knows when we may be suddenly alone.

Creative activity of whatever kind is a never-failing

source of deep fulfilment. Many forms of creative expression not only may but must be carried out in solitude. I must be alone to write — and this book is the result of several weeks of utter solitude spent at my cottage on the rocky shores of Canada's Severn River. How good a touch of friendship feels when I take a day or two for a breather and either visit a friend or have one visit me!

I can never thank God enough for the gift of creativity he has given me. It does an enormous amount to draw the sting from my being single. Or is my being single, perhaps, the reason for any depth and richness the gift may have? Who can tell? God has his own ways of meeting his children's needs. All I know is that I find great fulfilment and release, as well as plenty of discipline-demanding hard work, in the exercise of creativity. I think many single people may not have looked within themselves to see if God has implanted some latent gift of creativity which he meant them to develop and in so doing to assuage their own thirst and to pour rivers of living water to refresh his people everywhere. As Paul counselled Timothy, "Stir up — fan into flame — the gift that is in you"!

Belonging to a good church fellowship is another source of fulfilment. Single people should seek till they find one that meets their needs, then settle down and become part of it. Few churches are geared to single people, although things are improving somewhat in this regard. But if you do not get all you need, get what you can, and look to God to supply the rest in other ways. He will — often richly and unexpectedly. Meanwhile, you will find that giving out what you have is a source of fulfilment in itself. Get in somewhere and put down roots. Above all, do not drift from place to place, with responsibilities and fellowship nowhere!

Christian service, carried out in love for Christ and in obedience to his command, cannot fail to bring fulfilment. Here the single person, whose spare time may be largely his own, may perhaps find more fulfilment than some of his married friends. To serve for Jesus' sake, to touch lives for him, to build up others in the faith, to minister through word or song or deed — these are among life's richest fulfilments.

One of the hardest things about being single is that, lacking children, we have no stake in the future. One by one the roots of home, family and friends are torn up by the passing years. Our married friends are deeply involved with their grandchildren now, alert, keen, watching the unfolding of new life with incredible absorption. For them, the gaping holes caused by life's uprootings are filling in. For single people, this is not so; there is no natural healing for their inner devastation.

The knowledge that God's Spirit has worked and is working through me to reproduce or nourish his life in someone else is the one joy and strength I know that can reach into the void of human need and breathe the balm of fulfilment in place of barrenness. "They shall still bring forth fruit in old age," he has promised. And this, along with the privilege of knowing him and doing his will, God denies to none of his children.

How can you find fulfilment if you don't marry? Bring your needs to God and seek your fulfilment in him. Use your common sense to help yourself in practical ways. Be prepared to work hard, to assume responsibility, to take risks. Learn to be a warm and trustworthy friend. Then trust God to work out just that kind and quality of fulfilment that he knows your needs require. You will not be disappointed.

12
Relinquishment

Dr John White of the University of Manitoba, a practising psychiatrist there, until recently also a pastor, and a former missionary to Latin America, makes an interesting point in his recent book, *Eros Defiled.* He uses the term "sexual fasting" to describe the celibacy accepted as part of Christian discipleship. I prefer to call it "relinquishment", since "fasting" implies an eventual termination of the single state which most single people will never know.

In his chapter entitled "Your Urges and How You Experience Them", he explains psychologically how our attitudes can so influence our bodily appetites that a man fasting voluntarily will feel no hunger pangs while the same man, deprived of food by force, will suffer intolerably. He applies this principle to sex. Then he continues:

But what of single men and women and of all those for

whom the hungers of sex cannot be satisfied? What of those who twist and turn in restless half sleep haunted by fantasies that mock and inflame them?

> There *is* such a thing as sexual fasting. Many people, I am well aware, are not able to find it, but it exists.
>
> Just as the fasting person finds he no longer wishes for food while the starving person is tortured by mental visions of it, so some are able to experience the peace of sexual abstinence when they need to. Others are tormented. Everything depends upon their mindset or attitude. The slightest degree of ambivalence or double-mindedness spells ruin.
>
> I cannot stress this principle enough. Neither hunger for food nor hunger for sex increases automatically until we explode into uncontrollable behavior. Rather, it is as though a spring is wound up, locked in place, ready to be released when the occasion arises. And should that occasion not arise (and here I refer especially to sex), *I need experience no discomfort.* [Italics his.]

To this I must add my word of witness. For over forty years I have practiced such relinquishment, and I have proved the truth of this statement. I never understood the psychological rationale behind my experience until I read this book; thank you, John White, for giving my knowledge of God vocabulary and validity! But I have known God's faithfulness in this matter all my life. No one who comes to him in sexual relinquishment will find him to fail.

Dr White goes on to affirm another psychological truth which, if we are honest, most of us will also have discovered for ourselves:

If I am sensitive to the Holy Spirit in my daily walk, I will discover that it is perfectly possible to obey God. It may be painful to do so, but it is always possible. For instance, God may be dealing with me on the issue of forgiveness and be making me aware of my resentment towards my wife. I may not *want* to forgive. But if I want to, I can. To say to me, "Now *try* to forgive her," only gives me an out — "But I *have* tried and I can't." God says: "Forgive!" And though I may hate to, I *can.*

There is no question as to whether I *can* obey or not. When God puts His finger on something, I can.

Relinquishment is not a state at which we arrive suddenly, nor once and for all. It is a slow pilgrimage, and there are many stumblings and bruisings along the way. Although it may have a clearly-remembered beginning, it may also come about as the result of a slowly-growing awareness of God and his unfolding plan for our lives. It will have to be renewed again and again, even many times in a single day. To quote Frederick W. H. Myers: ("St Paul"):

> Let no man think that sudden in a minute
> All is accomplished and the work is done; —
> Though with thine earliest dawn thou shouldst
>   begin it
> Scarce were it ended in thy setting sun.

I think it is safe to say that everyone, at one time or another, has had a desire to be married. Most single people experience it constantly. Sometimes it is just a vague, lonely longing way down deep inside; sometimes, triggered by anything (or nothing), it erupts unexpectedly in an intense struggle which may last moments, hours, even weeks.

You meet it in the power of God. All of life is struggle; if it were not this one, it would be another. You just accept what is yours, offer it up to God, and get on with the business of living. Though I'm not really sure that I'd want this struggle to cease entirely — it's my badge of membership in the human race — it can be a problem.

But beside us stands the single Saviour. When he became our Redeemer, he did so absolutely. Taking our nature meant for Jesus knowing all the unspeakable longings of his single children. He experienced all our desires and tensions, and triumphed over them. And so we may, and so we must, and so we shall, through his strength.

For God is true. He cannot deny himself. He does not ask his children to endure more than flesh and blood can bear — more indeed than he himself has borne. He is faithful; he makes for us a way of escape that we may be able to do what he asks of us. He has written his laws of relinquishment deep within our psychological natures. Glad and total acceptance of his will is the key to victory and peace for the single Christian. As Amy Carmichael has so truly written, "In acceptance lieth peace."

13
Human Needs

So, you concede, it is possible to find fulfilment in other than biological ways. But what about my emotional needs, and my sexual needs apart from the purely physical? What about my need for companionship with the opposite sex, my need to love and to be loved, to share life, to belong?

These are valid questions. These are basic human needs. What answers are there for the Christian who is single?

There is no question but that chastity is required of us, chastity of mind and spirit as well as body. But does chastity mean the denial of our power to love? Does God demand that we negate our deepest nature, abdicate our truest being?

One celibate has described chastity not as a curtailment but as a *concentration of the power to love.* Another calls it a disciplining, a redirecting of that power; not the denial of our humanity, but a gift by means of which we are enabled to give ourselves heartwhole and without reserve to God and to other people instead of to just one person. Many who have willingly accepted lives of poverty, chastity and obedience in a religious vocation have found these things to be true.

This is a high calling indeed, and not one which many Christian single people would actually choose. But if we are his, it is for such a life that God, in effect, has chosen us. Those who, out of love to him and in acceptance of his sovereignty, embrace his choice will know his peace. They can confidently look to him for the meeting of their basic human needs; and to his faithfulness there are many who will bear witness.

How, then, may human needs be met?

Much of what was said in the chapter on fulfilment is applicable here as well. To quite an extent, what gives a sense of fulfilment also meets our emotional needs. As these vary somewhat from person to person, so will our outlets and sources of supply. There is no one path for everyone.

Most of us feel a need to belong — if not supremely to one person, then at least to a group where we are welcomed and esteemed and can find fellowship. Single people usually have to search out their own niches, even at times to create them; we seldom find them ready made. Even that basic unit, the family group, requires cultivation as brothers and sisters marry and a new generation replaces the older one. Especially is this true if only one family member has remained single. On the other hand, our careers, our mobility and our personal freedom work together to make it possible for us to sample many group situations and so to find those that best meet our own particular needs.

No one has to live without love — indeed, it is impossible to do so. As God's love is shed abroad in our hearts by the Holy Spirit, it must pour itself out in a nourishing stream to those around us. Our part is to let it go free, allowing God to direct its flow. He will bring into our lives those who most have need of our love, and conversely, will bring to us those whose love will most fittingly nourish us. Being human, we would prefer to choose those whom we would deeply love, and to restrict our deepest love to one person. If God has not given us that particular form of loving, it is only that we may know a greater concentration of our love on himself and a richer diversity and diffusion of love towards other people, never that we shall give or receive less love than our natures require.

Friendships cannot be overemphasized in the single life. They should be many and varied, always growing in depth, always increasing in number. (This last may take conscious effort as the years take their toll.) While some friendships will be closer than others, few, if any, should be exclusive — the pain can be almost intolerable if they should break down, which exclusive friendships often tend to do. And friendship, as well as group membership, provides fruitful ground for the sharing of life, which is something we all need.

Christian service meets our emotional and sexual needs even as we give ourselves freely to others in Jesus' name. Frequently it provides, if not opportunity for companionship with members of the other sex, at least the opportunity of working together and finding fellowship together in mixed company. This is something we all need, and which many of us do not have in our daily life and work. It is something of which our churches should be far more aware than most of them are. Most particularly, in service the joys of parenthood are opened wide to all who let God's Spirit use them to beget and nurture children in the faith. Spiritual fruitfulness is God's desire for every one of his children, and here there is no exception for single people.

Although for the Christian who is single chastity must supersede any sexual activity, the enjoyment of sexuality, in ourselves and in others, is God's rich gift to us all. It can become an infinite source of pleasure and repose to the single person, no matter what his situation.

I enjoy being a woman. Granted that this is still a man's world, that opportunities are often still unequal, that many doors are still closed to women — I still enjoy being a woman. All I need to do to know why is to contrast the somewhat pathetic manner in which most men seem to enter retirement with my own delighted arrival on that scene five years ago. I've never been so busy, so happy or so productive in my life.

I enjoy doing the things that women do — thoughtful, intelligent, creative women, anyway. I find great pleasure in caring for my home and garden, in handwork, sewing and other feminine pursuits — although many such activities are now being curtailed because of increasing arthritis. I work out the best and quickest ways of minimizing necessary routines so that I may devote more time to what I most want to do. I have innumerable ways of expressing my own sexuality and enjoying that of others.

The enjoyment of sexuality includes the enjoyment of our homes, a joy we share with all humanity and with most creatures as well. Single people should make and enjoy homes for themselves, accepting the responsibilities, the limitations and frustrations as well as the joys they entail, seeking to use them not only for personal happiness, but for Christ and his church as well. The choice of a home is a highly individual matter — a room in a hotel or a house of one's own — but there are very few people, if any, who do not need a home, even though some may not actually realize it. This is a need that single people can meet for themselves, and they are wise men and women who set about it early.

Tied in with the need for homemaking is the need of most adults for nurturing. Single people have many ways of meeting this need. They range all the way from those who content themselves with pampering a french poodle to those selfless souls who actually adopt or rear a child on their own. Don't think I am deprecating the keeping of a pet. God's furred and feathered friends are dear to me, a source of never-ceasing wonder and delight. I've shared my bed and board for many decades with a succession of distinguished cats. But indulging an animal must not be allowed to become a sublimation of the need to nurture. There is too much real need in this world for that. Most of us find a solution to this need somewhere between the two extremes.

I have always been grateful to God that he graciously met my own deep need to nurture by plunking me down in a classroom for thirty-eight years, most of them in the inner city. There I found plenty to do. Sometimes I thought it would be the death of me, but God knew what he was doing. Today I have children and grandchildren everywhere, and some of them are also children in the Lord. Meanwhile, my needs have been met. God is good.

No single person need be deprived of children. There are children everywhere for those less fortunate than I, children needing love and nurture, children who by their very being bring joy and richness and love in their wake. Single people who do not seek friendship among children just because they have none of their own are short-changing their own natures and failing in their Christian responsibility. They're also missing an awful lot of fun!

Along with the homing and nurturing instinct, indeed, almost a part of it, is the mating instinct. There is no outlet for this outside of marriage. The Christian who is single must relinquish it, and learn to live with it held firmly under God's control. But this is not as bleak a prospect as it may appear!

14 Married Friendships

Then am I to have no companionship at all with the opposite sex? You ask in dismay, and well you might. For we have been created in God's image in such a way that only as male and female together can we truly reflect God's glory. Indeed, it is not possible even to know ourselves aright except as increasingly we come to know the other sex. Where does this leave the Christian single person?

I used to think that it was much harder to be a single woman than a single man. Gradually I have come to change my views. It is probably easier for a single woman to find ways of enjoying her sexuality than for a man, if for no other reason than that there are so many of us; and homemaking, one of life's true delights, is an accepted form of expression for a woman. Nor do men really have free choice of a marriage partner, though certainly they have no lack of women among whom to choose. It is hard for a single woman to take her hands off her life and await

God's working concerning marriage, as I very well know; but a man is not really in a different situation. It is probably harder for him, for as a Christian he is not free to move on his own, yet must be sure enough of God's leading to be able to initiate a friendship which may lead to marriage, an awesome responsibility, surely! And since mature single men are few in number, it is probably harder for them than for us to find congenial companionship among themselves.

At the same time it will be hard for them to sustain deep friendships with most single women, who in all likelihood will view them only as potential mates. Occasionally a close friendship without evident intent to marry does exist between single people. When it does, other Christians should show sensitivity and restraint. They should refrain from jostling and speculation, give the Spirit of God freedom and allow the friendship to flourish. Many such a nourishing relationship has been done to death by well-meaning but heedless friends. All friendships need not lead to marriage. "Why aren't you married?" and "When are you going to get married?" are questions that have no place on Christian lips. Let God be God!

But in my experience, the best answer to the need of single people for companionship with the other sex lies in family friendships. Many people are afraid to allow a third person anywhere near the heart of a marriage. But if certain basic conditions prevail and such friendships are God-given, these fears are unfounded.

Single women must learn to see men as people rather than as potential partners, and to act themselves as people rather than primarily as females. When they do this, they will find deep and fulfilling friendships. I think that only women who have truly embraced singleness from God's hand are free to enjoy such friendships. It is surprising how many Christian men with strong, stable marriages are able to offer them.

God has entrusted me with many such friendships over the years, and they have been the single greatest blessing I have ever known. They are among life's richest gifts; I should not care to contemplate my life without them. I owe an inestimable debt of love and gratitude to those gracious men and women, God's true nobility, who have opened their hearts and homes to me in genuine friendships — some of which are now reaching into second and third generations. And in over forty years of enjoying married friendships, not one shadow has ever marred such a relationship, nor anything but death terminated one. The couples have ranged in age from twenty or more years my senior through my own age group and now include couples twenty or thirty years younger than I am.

Usually, though not always, I've met the man first. Maybe we worked together, or shared some form of Christian service or activity. We may have met through some mutual interest or friend. Friendships develop normally, and in course of time I am invited home to meet the family. If this didn't happen, I'd see to it that the working friendship remained on a very casual basis; if any other overture were substituted, the friendship would be dropped.

At this point the single person stands on the threshold of either a magnificent, heartwarming experience which can enrich her whole life, or a disaster. Which it becomes will usually depend on her.

To me, a true marriage has about it a personality of its own. It is the sum total of what the two partners are, of their children, and of what, under God, they have made of their life together. It is fascinating to encounter the personality of a marriage, and a rare privilege to draw near and come to know it. If it is this that attracts me to them rather than a pulling towards either partner alone, I am likely to be on safe ground. I must approach them as one person — which they are. If I cannot honestly and wholeheartedly do this, and especially if I am more attracted to him than to her, I must drop all thought of a warm relationship with that couple immediately. If she and I should happen to discover an affinity that he does not fully share, there is no reason why we cannot pursue a friendship on our own. The converse, of course, does not follow. No independent relationship between the husband and myself must be allowed to start.

Not that I might not enjoy doing certain things with one partner more than the other at some particular time — listening to new recordings with him if she is not especially musical; attending a play or a lecture about something in which she and I are interested while he is not; sharing her sewing project or acting as a sounding-board for his partly-finished manuscript. But my primary reason for wanting to be with them must be to enjoy the two of them together, along with their children; to find companionship and fellowship in a family setting; to warm my heart at the lovely thing that, under God, they have made of their marriage. True love and trust will flow in all directions as husband, wife, children and friend are enriched by the sharing of life. Perhaps you may meet some need for one or both partners, or for the children, that they are unable to meet for one another. As you give of yourself under God, your own deep needs are met in their love and friendship. With what exquisite grace does God set the solitary in families!

"But such situations don't exist!" you exclaim sadly. "There's not a wife anywhere who will let another woman come that close to her marriage!

It may be true that such women are few in number, but thank God, they do exist. Even today God has many marriages solid enough that single friends are welcomed and loved in their homes. I have never been without such friendships since my nineteenth year, although I was not always geographically close to them. Long before I could understand or articulate the foundation on which such friendships were built, I was experiencing their strength and beauty. It is only as I look back that I have learned to delineate them. I have never been able to thank God enough for those generous souls, particularly the women, who have made them possible.

"Why don't women like each other?" a puzzled young man asked me not long ago. The answer is not far to seek. Some of us are going to be left over in the game of musical chairs that is matrimony, and whether we realize it or not, we women are instinctive rivals. To a great many women, any other woman constitutes a threat.

But this is the world's way. Such an attitude should have no place among Christians, although alas, it is not unknown. But true Christian commitment frees us from such bondage. I accepted singleness at God's hand, if he should give it, early in my life; married friendships came to me only later. The one exception to this is the friendship of which I wrote in Chapter 3, where the pull was strongly towards the wife in any case.

The answer to married friendships, then, lies in commitment to God. Single people who know anything at all about friendship, and whose commitment to him is deep and real, will find that he brings into their lives, easily and naturally, couples of like commitment to God and to each other, his gracious gifts to his trusting child. Where true commitment exists, mixed friendships can flourish. There is seldom any need to speak of it; it shows in everything we do. I don't think I've ever discussed such commitment with my married friends; we simply recognize it in each other, and are mutually free to love and trust. God's people speak and understand his language. It's a great thing to belong to the family of God!

15
Practicalities

Family friendships do not burst full blown upon the single person. Like any other relationships, they grow slowly. If a deep friendship is to develop between a married couple and a single person, the single person must look well to the practicalities of the situation.

Most important, of course, her motivation must be transparently pure before God. If it isn't, she'd better drop out of sight until it is, maybe even permanently. On the other hand, single people need not torment themselves with unnecessary or false scruples. There are many good reasons for friendships between married people and single people. We must distinguish between accusation and conviction. The Holy Spirit convicts; it is Satan who accuses. If the Spirit convicts of sin, we must act on it at once; if the Accuser seeks to defeat us, we must silence him with the blood of the Lamb. This principle would apply here. Single people need not fear to accept family friendships from the hand of God.

The single woman who is a guest in a home must be very sensitive to the needs of the wife. It is largely on her that the burden of entertaining must fall. If she has young children, she will already have plenty to do; and because of her family responsibilities, most of the time you will spend with the couple is likely to be in her home. She must find pleasure in it as well as you.

The single woman should be alert to see how she can best fit into the picture. Unless she is specially requested to do so, she should not sit in the living room talking with the husband while the wife tries to get supper and cope with the late-afternoon tiredness of hungry children. She should see what needs to be done and quietly and efficiently set about doing it — whether it is feeding (or changing) the baby, gathering the little ones away from the kitchen for a quiet story, setting the table, putting toddlers to bed, helping with homework, hearing evening prayers, or whatever.

Before many visits have passed, she should be as familiar with her friend's kitchen as with her own, and know where things are kept. It is no mark of friendship to hide a busy mother's paring knife in some mysterious spot of her own invention; she should know where it belongs, and put it there. Quietly and unobtrusively she can prepare vegetables, make a salad, set out desserts, put away the shopping, clear up after a meal or otherwise make herself useful. Such a friend will find herself warmly welcomed by the wife.

Children respond immediately and wholeheartedly to the visitor who talks with them, tells them stories, reads aloud, teaches a song or helps make something — materials for which she has thoughtfully brought with her. The love of little children is of priceless worth. It should be cultivated for its own sake. Not only will it repay your investment of time and energy a thousandfold, it will pay dividends as well. When children love you they behave well when you are a guest. Parents do not fail to note this. Not everyone has this effect on their family; you will be invited back. Not that you would ever seek to use the children. Your interest and love should be genuine, and almost certainly will be — the children will see to that.

A word about gifts. If you are frequently invited for meals, a gift of fruit or freshly baked cakes is never out of place. But it is most unwise to bring gifts for the children each time you come. Children are acquisitive little creatures, and it is not good for them to learn to think of visitors in terms of expected gifts. An occasional small present is fine; but most of the time the better gifts to bring are ideas — stories to tell, games to play, topics to discuss. The last thing you want to do is to spoil your friends' children.

The thirteen-year old son of friends of mine answered the door when I arrived for dinner recently. When he saw me his dark eyes kindled. "I was so glad when Mum told me who was coming!" he exclaimed warmly. "Most folk who come here don't really pay much attention to us. You always talk to us, and you're so interested in what we're doing. We love it when you come!"

You could have knocked me over with a breath. This was a shy, sensitive, intelligent lad who seemed to keep very much to himself. He had never communicated so openly with me before. But of course I talk to those children! They're fascinating kids! Who wouldn't love them and be interested in them? They're magnificent people!

A single woman must guard against letting a married friendship become too important to her. Because its nourishing relationship meets a need for affection that she is unable to meet otherwise, almost subconsciously she may seek to make that friendship an exclusive one. There is no more certain way to kill it! Married friendships must be held under God, and held very loosely. The couple will have a great many independent friendships; so must you.

Privacy must never be invaded. Now and again it may be all right to drop in on a family unannounced, but such a visit should be the exception. In general, it is best to come when invited. Although you may sometimes be asked for holidays or other special occasions, you must not expect this to become a regular thing; perhaps you should even guard against this. The moment a friendship reaches the place where the couple begins to feel, "I suppose we ought to ask ...", that relationship is in trouble. Plan your own holiday activities often — like sharing your festivities with other single people. Your married friendship will be the healthier for it, and you may be a blessing to someone else.

The single woman must watch against any over-expression of the pleasure she finds in the family friendship. A warm, heartfelt "Thank you — I've enjoyed this so much!" is one thing; a constant reminder to others of your own aloneness is another.

In the first place, the truly committed Christian will not feel herself deprived; her satisfactions are not lacking, but merely other. In the second place, some compassionate married people feel very deeply for their single friends. Since they are already doing all they can for them in offering their friendship, they should not continually be reminded of their own privileged position as against the single person's. I have seen a young wife feel so keenly for me as actually to weep over my being single. I was deeply moved; but such moments can't really do much for the friendship, and they may create an emotional block. I don't want anyone to weep for me; I do not weep for myself. Certainly I must never precipitate such a response in another, nor make any sort of play for sympathy. This is not the climate in which friendships flourish.

Basically, I have felt it wisest to keep my own counsel concerning the happiness I find in married friendships. I have not tried to speak of the deep needs that they meet for me, nor of the vast love and indebtedness I feel, except on a very rare occasion—perhaps at a time of family crisis when such a word might minister healing. But my enjoyment of the friendship is open and whole-hearted, my pleasure in it plainly evident. Its joys and satisfactions are mutually experienced. If beneath the fun and laughter I am a well of gratitude that is infinite in depth, there are better ways of expressing it than in words. I have sought to find my own; each of us must do the same.

Single people should not be content to let the married couple bear all the burden of entertainment in their friendship. I don't think that it is easy for any one to prepare meals for guests, when most of us try to have something at least a little special. A single woman finds it hard to do after a day's work and a rough ride on the underground; a married woman after a hard day with a sick child.

The single woman should take her share of the entertaining. Not as often, perhaps, since few small flats are suitable for a lively family; but sometimes. A few pounds are wisely invested in disposable dishes, mugs that can be grasped by little fingers and won't easily spill, a pretty plastic tablecloth. Menus can be arranged with the mother in advance so there is no hassle over hated or unfamiliar foods. Precious bric-a-brac can be put safely away. Some sort of entertainment can be provided, or mothers may be asked to bring favourite toys, books or games. The flat may be declared a disaster area for a few hours, and a merry, if exhausting, time will be had by all. The mother will appreciate a meal she did not have to cook, even if you feel it is very mediocre.

Another time, of course, you can pay for a baby sitter and have the parents to a late, candlelit dinner by themselves. They will appreciate this even more — parents don't often have a meal away from their children.

Single people can invite families to picnics or barbecues, to rambles, swimming parties, ball games — the list of activities is endless. Once I spent a holiday Monday riding Toronto's underground, buses and street cars entertaining three lively youngsters aged 5 to 12. En route we visited any public building that took the children's fancy — the Royal York and King Edward Hotels; the Star Building; the old Union Station where they saw their first locomotive; the Harbour; a magnificent Roman Catholic church and the city's oldest Anglican cathedral; and the City Hall. Then we went home to sausages and ice cream in my kitchen. It takes almost nothing to make a child happy; I remember the day with genuine pleasure myself. And the parents had a whole holiday free.

If the wife is interested and you can afford it, to take her to an opera, a ballet, a concert or a film is a way of expressing gratitude for a friendship and for hospitality. Busy mothers tend to bypass such pleasures for themselves in doing things for their children. This is something you can do for her.

Or you can take a child to a performance of some artistic production to which he might show a latent sensitivity. I can still remember the joy I found in taking a musical twelve-year-old to her first performance of Handel's *Messiah* some thirty-five or more years ago. It was the beginning of a beautiful friendship which blesses me still.

Many single people, like myself, feel inferior when it comes to serving a meal to others who are more experienced and proficient at cooking than they are. I feel very much this way, and would avoid ever cooking for anyone else if I allowed myself to do so. I've never really liked cooking, and cooking for one person for over forty years has not done anything to make me like it any better. But I entertain my friends from time to time none the less. I have learned to make a few simple dishes fairly well, and fine music, candlelight or firelight, good conversation, love and laughter make up the rest.

I was voicing some of the thoughts in this chapter at a seminar one August day. When I spoke of being only an indifferent cook, I was sharply interrupted by a young man in the group, son-in-law of friends of mine.

"But that's nonsense!" he declared roundly. "You're a *terrific* cook! My parents-in-law have eaten at your place more than once, and they just *rave* about your food!"

I was speechless with astonishment. But there you have it. Fine music, candlelight, firelight, good conversation, love and laughter have remarkable powers!

16
Expressing Affection

How can affection be expressed between single people and members of the opposite sex? How, particularly, can it be expressed in married friendships?

When I was asked this question unexpectedly a few years ago, it caught me by surprise and I had no ready answer. The fact was that I had never really thought about it. I had enjoyed married friendships for several decades by then, and I had never felt that we lacked means of expressing our affection. I only knew that physical contact was not one of them.

I have tried to reduce to words some of the ways in which I have experienced satisfying expressions of affection. They are highly individual, of course. Perhaps they can do little for others except to suggest areas of thought which they might explore in searching for their own individual solutions. I speak here only of such expressions between opposites, since no problem exists between members of the same sex, or with children.

Christian people today, whether married or single, embrace very freely, both casually and otherwise. This is their privilege, within limits, and always under the Holy Spirit's control. I, too, know this freedom; but I very rarely use it.

My married friends have so profoundly enriched my life, and I stand in such reverence before the beauty and sanctity of their marriages, that I have not felt any desire for physical expression of the very real affection that we share. I have something much deeper and more satisfying than a mere physical embrace. It is too precious to risk losing it. I feel an immense debt of love and responsibility towards husbands, wives and children, and towards God the giver of our friendship. I am too conscious of the trust they have placed in me to want to encroach in any way on what God has not given. I do not care to jeopardize relationships that are at the same time both strong and fragile with anything as volatile as physical contact.

Nor do I feel restricted in any way that really matters. As John White says, "I need experience no discomfort." If a friendship is purely casual, I feel no desire for even a casual embrace. If it is deep and meaningful, I don't need one.

I find it interesting that although I have never discussed these feelings with any of my married friends, they have obviously been recognized and are matched by the feelings of the others concerned. A vast unspoken love and understanding engulfs us all. In all these years, no situation that could make such a discussion relevant has ever arisen. For this I praise God — and continue to exercise his gift of common sense. At the same time, I am not critical of what others do.

How, then, may affection be expressed?

Verbal expression is not ruled out, though good taste

and common sense will restrict it to a minimum. But delight in another's personhood and affirmation of his (her) uniqueness can be made in satisfying and more subtle ways than in words — which can sometimes prove embarrassing and may possibly be misunderstood.

"We love it when you come here, Margie!" the eldest of four keen-minded youngsters exclaimed at dinner in their much loved home where I was a frequent guest. "You're just about the only person we know who can put Daddy in a corner — and the *only* woman!"

I had the grace to blush, for the truth was that Daddy put me into a corner far more easily than I could corner him. He had a fine mind and a very quick wit; it was no easy task to get the better of him. He withheld the full strength of his rapier-like thrusts from most guests; but the moment I appeared, the battle was joined in full force. I enjoyed it thoroughly, and so did the onlookers. It took almost all I had merely to defend myself; but occasionally I was able to better him, to the huge delight of his family. He took his defeats with good grace, as I did mine; and our continuing battle of wits was one of the hallmarks of that friendship — and is now carried on with one of his grown-up sons, much to the delight of the son's own children.

I enjoyed our repartee for its own sake at the time, but it was only years later that I realized that it had also been a very real and satisfying way of expressing mutual affection — openly, freely, harmlessly, to be shared and enjoyed by all. Neither of us would unsheathe our verbal claws on anyone who could be hurt by them, but we were well matched. We showed mutual love and respect, and nourished and affirmed each other, by our relentless, good-humoured sparring.

I taught for a quick-minded principal once who treated

me in much the same way. He wouldn't have dreamed of treating another teacher on the staff to the sharp-tongued repartee he constantly directed at me, nor would another have dared to return it as I did. Our verbal exchanges broke the tedium or tension of many a long, hard day. We had an excellent working relationship, and our rather fierce banter only lightly disguised a very real affection and respect.

A pastor under whose ministry I once sat, whose wife and family I knew and loved, used to ring me sometimes on a Sunday afternoon to ask my opinion of his sermon that morning — something he might not ask of everyone. He expected an intelligent, completely candid answer; and after I got over the initial shock of inquiry, that is what he would get — a spontaneous analysis and critique that spared nothing. Each of us affirmed our esteem for and confidence in the other in this unlikely way — and I learned to keep my mind on the morning service!

Sometimes the same minister would discuss a projected series of sermons with me, seeking my reactions and suggestions. Occasionally he would ask me to write something for him — an article, song or poem for some special purpose. Since all these conversations took place by telephone, either from his office or his home, no one could doubt their transparency. Each of us enjoyed working at these levels with the other, and was nourished by the friendship.

An enormous amount of my best creative expression has had its origin in just such encounters — with close friends at first; then as my work became known, with editors and publishers whom I came to know only after they had put me to work at some project in which they needed my help. Some of these contacts have eventually led to good friendships; others remain good working relationships only. I thank God for them all. There is an infinite satisfaction in meeting another's need in some piece of creative endeavour; and it is probably safe to say it does more for me than it does for the other person. This book had its beginnings in just such a way, first as a requested article, then in book form; and I am grateful.

Affection has been expressed to me in a diversity of ways, each one uniquely suited to my particular personality and needs. Your experiences will be different, as you and I are different. But so personal is our God in his dealings with his children that each will be as uniquely yours as mine have been mine, and they will meet your needs just as individually.

Some of my friends may express affection by phoning their family greetings when passing through town. Some may keep the fires of friendship alight by assuming the role of family scribe. Some may ask advice about their children's educational problems. Some keep me abreast of their own professional or creative thought and endeavour. Some inform me when they are giving a lecture or a recital in my locality, occasionally sending tickets. Travellers may take the trouble to write that they have heard one of my hymns sung in some far corner of the world.

In return, I express my regard by attending their concerts even if the programme is mostly contemporary, which I don't always enjoy. I attend their lectures; I buy their records and books — I even read them! I apply all my teaching experience to their children's problems. Such in-depth communication is deeply satisfying.

Sometimes men express affection in amusing ways. More than one man has paid me what he considered to be the ultimate compliment by telling me that I think like a man. They are always somewhat baffled when I snort and toss the well-meant word back at them, informing them that I hope I think like an intelligent human being — male or female has nothing to do with it! However, I appreciate their good intentions none the less.

Friends delight to give gifts to one another. Married friendships may include gift-giving, but it will not take the usual form. I remember one friend with whom I used to exchange Bach chorales. Every time either of us found a new one in some musty, obscure hymnal, we would tell the other, and share our experiences in ancient text, tune and liturgy. One man enriched my life with his gift of Gilbert and Sullivan. Another gave me a magnificent gift in teaching me to understand Bach's devotional music. In return, I introduced him to the music of Mahler. Today, thirty years later, he and his family are still exploring its depths with delight, while I find more in Bach on every hearing.

Another friend taught me to read the church fathers and introduced me to church history. Yet another taught me to appreciate the writings of the Puritans and the Covenanters. I recognized that one friend had a latent gift of writing, and pestered him to write until in self-defence he wrote a book to shut me up. He so enjoyed the experience that he continued to write, and now is the author of several excellent books. Once, long ago, I helped a gospel pianist to discover the classics; and today he claims that that discovery was a turning point in his career. A gift may have many forms. Gifts of heart and mind will last long after other gifts are gone and forgotten.

Single people can express affection to their married friends by helping out in times of emergency, or by standing by when things are hard. I recall a summer more than thirty-five years ago when friends were moving and had to vacate the old house before the new one was ready. At the same time the wife was sitting with a dying mother. The day after school closed for the summer I collected the four children, aged 9 to 16, and cared for them for the next fortnight at their summer cottage while the parents got the new home ready. Since we were two miles by water from phone, post office, grocer's, or any other person, with only a leaky rowboat and our own young arms to maintain our link with humanity, it was quite an experience. I marvel now that the responsibility didn't overwhelm me. But I expressed my affection for my friends, and I still remember those weeks with pleasure — oil lamps, smoky cooking stove, mosquitoes, electric storms, mice, snakes, four starving kids and all!

Another couple I knew loved music, and would ask me to play for them at every opportunity. The husband's favourite selection was Handel's *Largo*. I was never particularly fond of it, but I expressed my affection for him by playing it hours without number, giving it everything I had. He and I had great fellowship in church history and hymnology, and his wife was especially dear to me. Why shouldn't I play *Largo* ad infinitum if it made him happy?

And so I could go on, incident after incident. Many of them go too deep to be told. These are some of the ways in which God has enabled me to experience affection: you must find your own. In ways like this I have found it possible to share life, to give and to receive love, and to be deeply happy and satisfied in doing so. Such experiences mean far more to me than an embrace from the men concerned could possibly mean. Indeed, in our situation, I suspect that not only might an embrace have added nothing of value to our relationship, it might have detracted from it or inhibited its growth.

Single people must learn to look for inner satisfactions in their married friendships, not outward expressions of affection or verbal endearments. Such satisfactions are the substance of which the embrace is merely the symbol. The symbol without the substance is worth nothing — as many an unhappy wife can tell. If God has given us the substance, what do we really lack?

I cannot feel that my experiences in regard to being single are unique. God has only done for me what he will do for any seeking single person, what he has done and is doing every day for thousands of his never-married children. Any uniqueness I may have lies only in the fact that I have thought deeply on these matters, and have sought to articulate some of my thoughts. I am always astonished to find how many single people have never sought God's release in their being single, nor ever considered that there could be any release outside marriage. God has many paths to joy and contentment for his single children.

17
Greener Pastures?

Single people who feel themselves unfulfilled are usually convinced that marriage would solve all their problems. The grass is always greener on the other side of the fence. Once in a while it does no harm to take a long, sober look at what's actually growing in other pastures.

There is much that is beautiful, of course. True Christian marriage is a lovely thing. But even within the finest of marriages there are tensions, often insoluble ones. It is not possible to escape them, to walk away from them or to forget about them. They must be lived with day after day, year after year, for ever. Nor do all marriages qualify as fine or even as good ones, although many of them do. All too many, alas, are far from being either. Even marriages between Christians may range from fair to poor to tragic. Such marriages hold more and more frustrations and unfulfilment as the years go by.

Single people whose married friendships have enabled them to see deeply into family life will not be so sure that married pastures are really greener than their own. There is no royal road to fusing two strong personalities into one. Certainly there is no easy way of rearing children. How grateful I used to be to close my classroom door at night! I loved my children and I loved teaching, but how glad I was to see my pupils go home — to have a few hours to myself, some life of my own!

Mothers know no such respite. The years that a young, active, intelligent wife must spend largely alone and confined to a houseful of tiny children, her whole horizon bounded by nappies, sleepless nights, tantrums and tears, must at times seem beyond human ability to endure. No matter how desired or how lovable children are, in their early years they are likely to be self-centred and demanding, small tyrants determined to enslave. Single people who only see them dressed up for Sunday seldom realize this. All honour to the parents, particularly the mothers, who survive these trying years and emerge with sanity and sanctity intact, a well-behaved, delightful family in their wake! I think there must be a special crown reserved for them. Children are one of God's special methods of fashioning adults out of immature grown-ups; and it is not an easy process.

Putting twenty-one meals a week on the table just for myself is a task to which I begrudge the surprising amount of time and energy it demands. How would I fare if I had to produce as many meals a day, every day, year in, year out, as countless mothers must? Not to mention keeping such a household clean, clothed, happy, healthy and harmonious; duly instructed in manners and morals, in the word of God and all else pertaining to life and godliness; co-operative, punctual, regularly attendant upon teachers, dentists, doctors, libraries, piano lessons, band practice, Sunday school and who knows what else! Should

I ever get anything else done in this world?

Children may be the source of life's richest delight, but they may also be the source of its deepest pain. Few families escape the griefs that come with children. Most of my contemporaries have experienced or are experiencing such sorrow in one form or another, either in their own children or their grandchildren. I think such anguish is the deepest the human heart can know. This kind of sorrow is one which God has graciously spared me. Single people should think long and hard about that side of parenthood.

And what of marriages where there is no communication between partners, no closeness, no companionship, no oneness, even though both partners are Christians? There is no one on earth lonelier than a lonely married person. They find no fulfilment in their marriage, yet are not free to seek it elsewhere. Instead they keep up a grim charade, going through the motions of life in community but living in utter isolation — and alas, their name is legion. Lonely single people are under no such bind. We should think realistically about these things when we pity ourselves because we are sometimes lonely. We may indeed experience more personal loneliness than the partners in a good marriage, but at least we are not always and only lonely, with no way of finding a solution to our loneliness.

What of a situation where two Christians marry, set up a Christian home, take up Christian work, perhaps, or maybe even go to the mission field. Then ten or fifteen years later, the husband's faith begins to erode. He starts to look to human wisdom rather than to the word of God. Gradually his faith breaks down altogether. He leaves Christian work, then leaves his wife as well, usually for another woman. With what unutterable anguish the wife must experience this death of all her hopes and trust! How she must fear for her children! How little did she dream that she would be left to rear them in the nurture and admonition of the Lord all alone! Such devastation can and does happen; but it cannot overtake a single person. We should consider this part of the total picture when we contemplate the greener pastures over yonder.

Once I was the only single person in a fellowship group of half a dozen married couples. They had taken me in when I had moved to their neighbourhood and been unable to find a more varied group. We had good times together, sharing at deep levels, although I was twenty years older than any of them.

During Bible study one night the leader chanced to allude to "our inability to admit to one another our loneliness or sense of alienation" as if he considered such a situation to be an accepted fact of life. I demurred, saying that I did not feel that this was so; I myself did not find it difficult to make such an admission on occasion. The five couples exchanged long, significant glances.

The leader gallantly elected to investigate the subject further, and asked for a yes or no answer from each of us. Out of the eleven present, I was the only one who felt I could voice such feelings, although all eventually admitted to suffering from them.

We were so mutually astonished at the results of our poll that we let down our collective hair and really thrashed the subject out. The upshot was curious. The married people felt that they could not express such feelings lest they should seem to be disloyal to their partners. I, a single person, had no such inhibition. If I needed to talk and could find the right person with whom to discuss a problem, I was free to seek help at any time.

On further thought, I realized that this was only one of many such inner freedoms that I had simply taken for granted. As a single woman, I have no one person to whom I can look for the meeting of my human needs. But I have deep relationships with many people — men and women, children and old folk, single people and married couples; so that I have many sources of supply. This friend meets this special need, that one another, a third, yet another. In a many-coloured tapestry of rich and varied hues God has woven my life together with many others. Each has his particular gift; we minister mutually each to other. There is scarcely a need for which I do not have a source of supply somewhere among the friends God has given me, and I am totally free to reach out for help when I need it.

In a sense, this applies even to sexual needs. Married people know one opposite in totality, and their needs are met in so far as they are able to cherish and nurture each other. The single person, though never knowing one person physically or in a depth comparable to marriage, may know many opposites in some depth, and with some of them find friendship at very deep levels. Though this will not meet all sexual needs, it can meet a great many of them; and it can contribute immeasurably to growth and happiness. This diversity of loving is a gift that many single people either never discover or simply accept as a matter of course, without appreciating its value. It is a freedom for which I am profoundly grateful, and one that has made me a very rich woman.

No one person can meet all his partner's needs. And needs change. Sometimes those who marry young find that while needs are met for a few years, growth takes place in diverse directions. A few years later they may not be able to satisfy each other at all; yet most of a lifetime may lie ahead. When a single person's needs change, so may his friendships. This freedom is a richer gift than many suppose.

The single person is also free to choose his friends. Most couples choose their friends among other couples, which means that four people, rather than two, must feel affinity. This can prove limiting. Often only one in each couple feels such closeness. Unless the other two are particularly broadminded, or even if they are, true friendship does not flourish. And if all four do desire friendship, there is always the possibility that too great a polarity between opposites can cause it to crumble.

Children can be distracting in a friendship. Ideas of child-rearing differ. One couple's permissiveness or rigidity can throw a severe strain on the other couple and so undermine the friendship. Or the parents may enjoy one another but the children may not. And even if all parties agree, as children grow their interests and activities begin to fan out in all directions. It becomes difficult for one family to remain cohesive, let alone two; and so the friendship falls into disrepair. Single people know greater flexibility in friendship, and have fewer distractions.

Contrary to popular married notions, most single people do not have more free time than other people. Any single person who holds down a job for forty years or more, perhaps commuting long distances twice daily, and caring for a home and meals without benefit of a wife — *what* wouldn't I have given for a wife when I was teaching! — has very little free time. And single people often have aged or infirm relatives to care for, even provide for, as well.

What single people may have more frequently than married people is flexibility within what free time they have. They can often adjust their personal schedule to fit a special need, since they have only their own and their working needs to be considered, not family ones.

But all this is purely relative. Some married people can adjust their time more easily than some single people, especially those with wives who keep the wheels of life oiled and running smoothly.

Greener pastures? Perhaps; perhaps not. It's likely they are much the same. Within marriage or the single state there are different freedoms, different sets of restrictions, different rewards, in each situation; some better, some worse, many imponderable. Advantages and disadvantages? What does it matter? For the Christian, life is not a matter of personal advantage, but of God's gift.

For the Christian who has embraced God's sovereignty, the choice is God's; and the result, whatever that choice may be, is rejoicing. In him is our joy and peace. If he gives marriage, then in marriage we rejoice. If he gives singleness, we rejoice in being single. In whatever state we are, we know contentment.

Meanwhile, there is work to be done — work in which married couples and single people must stand side by side. Let's join hands and get on with the job!

18
Non-persons?

What do the Scriptures have to say to single people? Specifically as single people, almost nothing — although all that the gospel offers in general terms is for all. In the culture of biblical times, the single state did not exist. Jewish men were required to marry — indeed, John Pollock contends that Paul could not have been a bachelor as is generally supposed because he could not have been a member of the Sanhedrin unless he were married and a father (John Pollock, *The Apostle*, Hodder & Stoughton).

Women's status in biblical times was simply that of a chattel, a piece of property. There was no such thing as a single woman. Girls were married off when little more than children — what father would forgo the bride-price longer than necessary? Under Mosaic law Hebrew women fared better than their counterparts in heathen lands; but even so, the state of women in Old Testament times arouses no envy in my breast. And in New Testament times things seem to have been very little different.

Many single men and women are dismayed by the scriptural silence concerning the single state; and many women, married as well as single, find themselves crushed by their seeming scriptural nonentity. They feel like non-persons, as if in God's sight they don't exist. Sometimes they entertain a secret — or public — controversy with him about it, maybe even letting it poison their whole lives. I must admit myself, that while agreeing "Shall not the Judge of all the earth do right?" I have sometimes felt that God was perhaps just a *little* hard on single women! How are Christian women, particularly single ones, to cope with the somewhat shattering enigma of their seeming scriptural nonentity?

Let me state categorically here and now that I don't pretend to have the answers to such questions. These things are as much a mystery to me as to you. But I can't say that I've ever been deeply troubled by them. Certainly they do not cripple me emotionally, spiritually or otherwise. I have good reason for this freedom: I find it in the scriptures, and in Jesus Christ.

I am neither a biblical scholar nor a student of the Bible's original languages nor its ancient history. I'm not qualified to split hairs on fine points of scripture. But I have read the Bible thoughtfully for more than half a century, and have tried to learn as much about it as I can. More particularly, I have sought to know the God whose sovereign self-disclosure the Bible is. My conclusion is that the God whose nature and character I have found so richly portrayed in his word and so true in my experience, is not a person who puts anybody down, whether man or woman. The so-called "problem passages" of scripture must have some better explanation.

What it is, I do not claim to know. The increasing

research being done by modern scholars, some of whom are women, may cast new light on some things. Certainly there were no women theologians among the early church writers. This, along with the cultural patterns of the day, may explain a certain bias in their concerted viewpoint. Certainly there are signs of prejudice on some points, a few of which are now being seen more clearly. Satisfying answers to some questions may emerge from further independent studies.

But it is possible that "a cloud of unknowing" may always hover over some issues. Some tensions may have to remain unresolved. The scriptures will never become so transparent as to make faith unnecessary. I think that women, as bearers and nurturers of the race, homemakers and teachers, have always needed more faith than men. This "cloud" may be one of God's ways of developing in women the greater depths of faith they need in order to transmit true knowledge of God to ensuing generations. Let us not allow it to block God's purpose for us!

I think that Satan has a strong personal stake in keeping women upset and emotionally crippled about such things. His head was to be bruised and his ultimate destruction brought about by the seed of the woman. Jesus was Son of God and of Mary — no man had anything to do with his birth and victory. Enmity was put between Satan and the woman.

We may not have realized this, or we may have forgotten it, but I don't think that Satan has. If he can keep women from finding their identity and freedom in Christ, just keep them busy fussing or fretting about less important issues, he can in some measure strike back at his mighty conqueror. Again, let us not allow him to block God's purposes for us!

New books on women in Scripture are constantly appearing. Two excellent ones, both of which I have found helpful, offer differing viewpoints: *In Search of God's Ideal Woman* by Dorothy Pape (InterVarsity Press) and *Let Me Be A Woman* by Elizabeth Elliot (Tyndale House Publishers). I suggest that concerned women read them both. They will repay careful study.

In the Old Testament we see women almost exclusively as wives and mothers. But on the few recorded occasions where God gave a woman an important position, as prophetess or judge, he gave her equal treatment in every respect with men of like status. In one case the woman actually received preference. Look up Huldah and Deborah in a modern Bible dictionary, and study the scripture passages about them. In general, God accommodated himself to the cultural conditions of the times in which the scriptures were given; his spokesmen were mostly men. But when he used a woman, as he sometimes did, he treated her exactly as he treated her male counterparts. To me, this has enormous significance. I found it a very healing truth when I first discovered it.

Jesus' treatment of women was revolutionary for his times (see Dorothy Pape for an enlightening and detailed study). I don't know how any woman can feel "put down" or "non-existent" once she realizes the significance of Jesus' attitude towards her and finds her identity in him. Both Jesus and the apostles gave women a much more important place in their ministry than is generally conceded — again, see Dorothy Pape's fine studies in this matter. True, no disciples and no apostles were women — such a break with the prevailing cultural tradition would have proved so revolutionary as to impede or even prohibit the spread of the gospel — which was the Spirit's first concern in those crucial days. But there were women in the upper room on the day of Pentecost, and they were filled with the Holy Spirit and commissioned along with the men. Women travelled with Jesus, and with Peter and Paul, and shared in their ministry, some — such as Priscilla — in really important ways. That in itself was nothing less than a radical innovation for the time, and has profound significance. I believe that there is more freedom offered to women in the scriptures than anywhere else on earth — more than we have ever dreamed of, much less sought to make our own. Most of us have never really tried to find it.

The "difficult passages" of the epistles remain problems. I believe that most of them can be explained in terms of the general culture, or of certain local situations that prevailed at the time and among the people to whom the letters were addressed. Further research may verify and enlarge upon such understanding of some passages. The reasons for seeming prohibitions voiced in other passages may be lost in antiquity and never recovered. The scriptures will never dispense with the need for faith.

At the same time, certain things concerning the relationship of man and wife are clearly grounded in creation, are verified by Jesus, and are reflected in the church. These are universal and unchanging. This is for our good, and I accept it without question. So will any woman who has had to make a life, a home and a sphere of service for herself entirely alone.

Matters of interpretation, however, must bear close and careful scrutiny as we honestly seek to discover what God is really saying to his people today. Cultural patterns must constantly be investigated, not only those of ancient times, but just as necessarily, our own. I think that our culture has allowed as much Pharisaical accretia to accumulate around certain passages in recent centuries as in early ones, and it is just as crippling to the free movement of the Spirit among us now as then. We must be freed from all such man-made additions to the law before we can rightly discern God's truth and his will for our day, and do it.

Single people who seek their identity in the word of God will find an infinite number of passages that minister particularly to their needs — verses written, as it were, especially for them. The tender yearnings of Jehovah over Israel, where he portrays himself as a faithful husband weeping longingly over his erring wife, give us an intimate picture of the character of the one with whom we have to do. Countless verses throughout the scriptures delineate God in very human terms. He is the one who pities his children as a father (Psalm 103:13); who comforts them as a mother (Isaiah 66:13); who offers them the breasts of his consolations (Isaiah 66:17); who rejoices over us with joy and singing (Zephaniah 3:17); who calls himself our husband (Isaiah 54:5); who promises that the barren shall bear children (Isaiah 54:1); who sets the solitary in families (Psalm 68:6). He is the one who knows our frame and remembers that we are dust (Psalm 103:14); who is touched with the feeling of our infirmities (Hebrews 4:15); who holds our times in his hand (Psalm 31:15); who chooses our inheritance for us (Psalm 47:4). He is our beloved, our bridegroom, our friend (Song of Solomon 5:16).

Why is so much of the imagery of these verses, and innumerable others, sexual in nature? Because it is universal language that all humanity needs and understands — and so do we. God means his children to look to him for the fulfilment of their human needs. The great, pulsing Father-Mother-Lover-Saviour heart of God holds all that the human heart — even the single human heart — can desire. If more Christian women spent less time worrying about their "rights" and more time contemplating the nature of God and drawing on his sufficiency for their needs, we'd all be happier. There would be fewer negative, unfulfilled, self-pitying people, whether single or married, and more self-giving, productive, positive Christians living everywhere.

Put down? Nonentity? Non-existent? Enslaved? Not if you know the God of the scriptures and take your identity and freedom from him!

19
So Love Has Come At Last

So love has come to you at last, and you are reeling under its powerful impact. It would be sheer joy if he were free and God had given him to you. But he isn't, and God hasn't. Somehow you find yourself loving one of your married friends, or a non-Christian, or someone else you know is not for you.

The awareness has probably dawned on you slowly. You didn't believe it at first, but now you have to admit it's true. You can't explain it. You'd never meant anything like this to happen. You have always sought to honour God in all your friendships, including this one; and as far as you know, you've been careful. Yet here you are, a follower of Jesus Christ, faced with the shattering realization that you love someone God has not given you, someone you can never hope to have. What do you do now?

What are your alternatives, and what are their consequences?

You can consider some sort of dalliance, of course — keeping within the law, perhaps, while indulging your desire in seemingly harmless ways. Or you can hug your bittersweet secret close and gloat over it in private, seeking comfort in some half-world of fantasy. Or you can do now what you know in your heart is the only right thing to do, and forswear before God, totally and irrevocably, your human desire for this man.

No matter which alternative you choose, the consequences will be painful. It is not easy to abjure a human love. But to cherish or to indulge it will prove more painful in the long run. Fantasy is a bitter, barren and isolating mistress. Indulgence is guilt-producing and self-destructive. It can hold only anguish for you and heartbreak for others; and it is bound to do despite to the name of Jesus Christ.

For the true Christian, there is only one answer to a love that may not be, and that is to give it back to God. True, this is more easily said than done. But if in the clear light of the scriptures it must be done, then in the power of the Holy Spirit it can be done. And now that you know where you stand, the battle must be joined immediately.

Probably the most intense part of your personal anguish at present is the sense of guilt you feel. To find yourself in the throes of a forbidden love is to feel guilty, whether you actually are guilty or not. You find it almost impossible to pray. Just when you need God most, you can't seem to get through to him. Though you may spend hours trying to draw near, your sense of guilt bars the way. You come to him in repentance again and again, but somehow you never quite feel forgiven. And try as you may to pray about other things, this one subject keeps recurring like a spot on an ever-revolving wheel. Your mind seems to focus on only one thing. You simply don't know what to do next.

Your first task is to deal with the guilt question.

If in fact you *have* been guilty of any complicity that has helped to bring about your present situation, you must face up to it. Did you, consciously or unconsciously, seek to attract his attention in any way? Were there no straws in the wind that could have helped you to prevent this happening? Did you really not see them, or did you in fact choose not to see them? Such questions must be faced ruthlessly and honestly. If you must answer "yes", then the guilt you feel is real guilt.

There is only one remedy for such guilt — the blood of Jesus. For his sake, God offers you immediate forgiveness and cleansing, and a restoration of full fellowship with himself. Your part is to come to him in confession and repentance; to tell God that his will is good and your action wrong. True repentance must include a definite and conclusive turning away from anything and everything that could contribute to further sin. Your wrong relationship must be broken off completely.

Remember, though, that your experience of God's forgiveness does not depend on whether you *feel* forgiven or not. If you have met his conditions, then he has already fulfilled his promise to you — you are forgiven, and your sin is forgotten. You simply accept this by faith and act accordingly. Jesus carried your guilt — there is no need for you to continue to bear it. To do so is to dishonour God.

It is possible, however, that you may not be suffering from real guilt at all, but from false guilt, which is quite a different matter. You may be quite innocent of any wrongdoing concerning this love. For most people, falling in love is something that happens to them. It can happen without their even being aware of it. Love itself is not wrong. The discovery of an impossible love is a serious matter calling for resolute action, but it is not necessarily a source of true guilt.

"The Spirit convicts; the Enemy accuses": so writes John White in his excellent chapter on temptation in *The Fight*—a book you may find very useful reading just now. If the Holy Spirit convicts you of sin, nothing but confession, repentance and renunciation will remove your guilt. But if after you have done this you are still tormented by a sense of guilt, you must recognize the voice of the Accuser. The creation of false guilt is the goal of the Accuser. With it he seeks to render believers useless to God. You will not get rid of false guilt by imploring God to forgive you, but by turning to face the Accuser and claiming Christ's authority over him until he flees from you. The soul that is sensitive to the Spirit of God will in time learn to discriminate between his conviction and the accusations of the enemy, and act accordingly.

Some of your guilt may have arisen from erotic feelings which accompany your love. Erotic feelings, like love, are not in themselves wrong. Perhaps here we should consider the meaning of the words "desire" and "lust". Whether consciously or unconsciously, most of us tend to equate these words in our minds. Even certain passages of scripture seem to use them interchangeably, although this is not reflected in the teaching of the scriptures as a whole. As a result, we single people may be tormented with guilt when we become conscious of physical desire. Since we are human, such consciousness is and will continue to be a constantly recurring experience; hence our guilt is likely to be compounded rather than resolved. And Satan, who knows our nature so well, will never cease to accuse us and try to cripple God's work in and through us by means of false guilt.

Sexual desire, with its accompanying erotic feelings, is not wrong. It is normal and right and good, a part of the way in which we have been created in the image of God. Along with it comes a vast capacity for loving, for giving, for communicating, for cherishing, for expressing tenderness and compassion. We accept it with gratitude as a God-given gift we should not want to be without. There is nothing sinful about it. But we have to learn to live with it and to control it; and we must learn to endure temptation in this area of our lives, and to overcome it.

Lust, on the other hand, may be described as a perversion of desire, as desire twisted, or pulled aside from the true. Desire becomes lust at the point where it is exalted to the place of deity. When desire says "I must have what I want, whatever it may cost to others or however it may affect my relationship with God", then it becomes lust.

Lust may be experienced by married people as well as by single people, and often is. Whenever desire is satisfied selfishly, at the expense of another or in doubtful purity, lust has conceived and brought forth sin (James 1:15). Married and single people alike must war on lust continually, although they will do so in different situations.

Nor is lust purely a sexual matter. It may be experienced in any of our natural appetites — in hunger, thirst, our need for sleep or exercise, as well as in our desire for sex. It is a matter of heart and mind no less than deed (1 John 2:15-17; Matthew 5:28). It is lust that seeks to distort our natural love of the beautiful until we make beauty a source of idolatry. Lust flourishes in our pride and ambition — do we not speak of a lust for power or money? And lust in all its forms is sin in God's sight.

We single people must seek to free ourselves from the false guilt with which the Accuser tries to saddle us concerning physical desire, and to recognize the ways in which for us desire may give rise to lust. Married people who have not done so should consider what constitutes lust for them. Then we must all fight it, resisting the Adversary in the power of God until we overcome him.

If you find yourself in the unenviable position of loving the wrong person, your first task is to settle the sin question and to get rid of all guilt, whether real or imagined. If your situation is known to others, restitution may be necessary; if not, lay everything before God and deal as he directs. Then you must begin the long, painful process of separating yourself emotionally from your love, and pursue it relentlessly until the work is done. No one can help you with it — you are going to have to do it alone.

Here there is no set of guidelines to help you; you will have to seek out your own. If you can drop out of sight without creating a situation that might prove even more awkward than your present one, it is probably best to do so. In general, the less you see of him anywhere in the future, the better for all concerned. Especially is this true if there has been mutual attraction, or if he is aware of your feelings for him. But because any sudden change in your habits might attract unwelcome attention and so defeat its purpose, it may be wise to make changes gradually until eventually you can slip away unnoticed — not the pleasantest prospect, to be sure, but one you may have to embrace nonetheless.

There is no way of relinquishing any love without suffering, and suffering intensely. But here you are doing business at deep levels with God himself. You are seeking to free yourself from an emotional attachment which he has not given you. You are his disciple, and you have no choice but to obey him, cost what it may. This is a matter of spiritual life and death, and radical surgery, even amputation, may be required. If these words sound hard and unfeeling, it is because the ruthless action facing you now *is* hard, even agonizing. And no amount of feeling is going to help you out — only the doing of this difficult deed.

But no one who relinquishes a human love for the love of Jesus will go uncomforted. God has pledged himself to meet our every need — and this must include our emotional needs. "I will not leave you comfortless", he has promised; "*I will come to you.*" "I, even I, am he that comforteth you ...." "As one whom his mother comforteth, so will I comfort you; *and ye shall be comforted*" (John 14:18; Isaiah 51:12; 66:13). If you stand today in special need of comfort, then he speaks these words to you.

"*I will come to you.*" Who can enter the secret places of another's heart and need? Who can understand his longings, heal his wounds and touch his spirit with peace? Not the dearest of earthly loves; and certainly not this present love of yours. But Jesus can and will: "*I will come to you.*" We may know his presence in the innermost depths of our soul, that hidden centre where not even the truest of human loves can fully penetrate. And one day you, too, will bear witness to the wonder of God's sufficiency in the midst of your pain, and will exclaim with the psalmist, "In the multitude of my thoughts within me, thy comforts delight my soul" (Psalm 94:19).

For God has not allowed this experience to come into your life to no purpose — to rob you, cheat you, or deprive you of happiness and good. No experience of love is ever lost. Through experiencing human love our hearts may be opened to receive God's love more fully. You can withdraw into the prison of self-pity and despair, or you can open your heart and let God flood it with love and compassion, with understanding of yourself and of others, with warmth and wisdom and wonder that will enrich your own life and overflow in healing and nurture to others. Do not cast away this opportunity to grasp the wealth of love that God is offering you today.

Anyone may experience God in this larger manner, of course, and many Christians do. But our humanity is such that we are all too likely to settle for human satisfactions unless we are pressed by some special need. And it is in knowing God that we single people may have an advantage over our married friends. Our enormous need throws us wholly upon him for supply. If we are minded to grow in grace, we have a powerful impetus to open our hearts to God and to receive him.

Life's greatest times of spiritual growth often coincide with its times of greatest need. Your present situation holds great spiritual significance for you. Embrace it, and wring from it all the experience of God that he longs to have you discover.

20
To What Purpose?

"To what purpose is this waste?" Single people would not be human if at some time or another this cry was not wrung from their hearts. There are times when such a depth of loneliness wells up within us, such a sense of alienation engulfs us, that we cry out to God in anguish at the apparent waste of his endowments. Rich personalities that know no blending with another; brilliant minds that know no kinship; full hearts that find no union with their kind — to what purpose is such waste?

Moments like this are few, fortunately, and of short duration. They decrease both in frequency and in intensity as we mature in Christ, and lose much of their power to shake us. But for most of us, such times of desolation do exist. We never know when we may suddenly be called to do battle with them.

What do the scriptures have to say to such a question?

Those who come to know the nature of God will early realize that in his economy there is no waste. Redirecting, rechannelling, even recycling, yes; but waste, no. "In the mathematics of God there are percentages greater than one hundred", as Margaret Avison has written.

God has innumerable ways of absorbing into the life of his church every gift that he has given and perfected in his children. He at whose command the disciples gathered up the fragments of loaves and fishes lest any part of his miracle be wasted, is still the husbandman of his gifts. No creative mind, no warm personality, no loving heart is lost; all have their place and usefulness in his eternal purpose.

Scriptures sum up the meeting of human need under the general term of *comfort.* God calls himself the God of all comfort. He tells us that he comforts us in all our afflictions that we may be able to pass on to others the comforts he has given to us (2 Corinthians 1:3,4).

Man's necessity met by God's sufficiency equals God's comfort. But comfort is given in order to be passed on. From the loneliness and longing of the single heart, God is fashioning comfort to nourish his church.

It is only to those who lack comfort that comfort is given. Hence our need qualifies us in a special way to be ministers of God's mercy. God equips us for the task as he comforts us day by day, harnessing the torrent of our suffering, as it were, to turn the millstone of his gracious, inscrutable purpose, and so feed his flock. If the torrent were to be released, there would be no comfort and no nurture. It is only *as we share* (present tense) in Christ's sufferings that we share in his comfort and so in his ministry (2 Corinthians 1:5). It does not seem to be possible to comfort another from memories of past sufferings; there must be active and present participation if there is to be nourishing comfort. But active participation is not waste.

Harriet Eleanor Hamilton King has written (in "Sermon In The Hospital" from *The Disciples*):

> Measure thy life by loss instead of gain;
> Not by the wine drunk, but the wine poured forth;
> For love's strength standeth in love's sacrifice;
> And whoso suffers most hath most to give.

It is to such a life of nurture that God calls his single people. Not the call we would have chosen — true; but the call we have. Life must be poured out one way or another — it cannot be contained. We single people will either overflow in service for God or in pity upon ourselves. The choice is ours, and it cannot be evaded. What we choose will determine our quality of life not only on earth, but also in heaven.

John White writes in *Eros Defiled*:

> I do not know the specific thing the world and the kingdom of God expect of you. But I know that it will be a unique thing that you alone can offer. I know that it will arise from abundant suffering. And I know also that it will spring from a superabundant glory of consoling peace.

21
Single People and the Church

How has being single affected your relationship to the church? I am often asked this question. My answer will differ from yours, and yours from the answers of others. This is an individual thing. Much depends on the situations and the persons involved, which may vary widely.

In general, however, I must say that I feel that the church has done less than it should for its single people, especially women. By its very nature the church should be more sensitive to human needs than anyone else, and should take the lead in seeking to meet them. Yet in many ways the church is the hardest place for a single woman to gain acceptance as a person and to find a suitable outlet for her gifts; and many married women seem to feel the same. Single men may fare a little better, especially if their abilities qualify them to assume responsibility; but many women find a thorny problem in their relationship to the church. A creative woman, even if she has no desire for prominence, may have a really rough time.

A far greater stereotyping of roles seems to exist in most churches than in the working world. Whatever her ability, experience or spiritual gifts, a woman is usually expected to fill a traditional female role in the church, generally in the kitchen or with babies or young children. She may not be especially well suited to this, and other work which she could do better may be crying out for workers; but no matter. Assignment of tasks is decided by governing bodies who until recently have been entirely male and in many places still are. Not all of them are well suited to the work of government, although most would be loath to give it up. It never occurs to them to look at a woman as a Christian uniquely gifted by the Spirit for the good of the whole body of Christ. She is seen merely as a subject for a female role-assignment, which has been pre-determined by others (male others!) and long ago set in cement. Many women, particularly single women who stand side by side with men in the working world, find this difficult to accept. "The church has a responsibility to take the gifts and ministries of women seriously," writes Linda Le Sourd, "for they are given by Christ for the benefit of all believers."

This is not to suggest that we may go beyond scripture. The Bible lays down certain ground rules about such things which we ignore at our peril. No true Christian woman who knows the scriptures really wishes to change them. But the same scriptures also portray a vast freedom for all Christians, not excluding women, that is only dimly envisaged by and is rarely experienced in our church of today. Many of our ruling elders are totally unaware that such freedom exists. Such a situation calls for change.

Differences of interpretation of some scriptures exist between good and godly men of equal devotion and biblical scholarship. We know that many of the interdictions of the epistles were based on cultural or local circumstances which no longer obtain, and hence are not binding upon all Christians for all time. But honest opinions differ as to just what must be obeyed literally and what may be applied spiritually. It is possible there may always be dissent over some of these things.

In addition to this, most of us are victims of our own culture. Many of those who refuse to allow women any part in government or teaching would be totally unable to give a comprehensive scriptural rationale for their attitude. They do not know the scriptures as a whole; their ideas are based on a few isolated texts and, far more than they know, on the traditions and customs of their own background. Pharisaism did not die with the first century.

It is not my purpose to go into these and other related questions here. I merely wish to suggest that if contradictions seem to occur in scripture, then serious study is called for. But it must be unprejudiced study, and it must carry with it a willingness to obey any new light that may be given. The scriptures do not contradict themselves. Their inherent harmony must be discovered and their apparent discrepancies so reconciled.

We must face the fact that we may not have enough source material still extant to answer all our questions. We must learn to function as one body nonetheless. We should be slow to set forth any one interpretation as the only right one and to demand that everyone else conform to our opinion. We must bow before the Spirit's sovereignty and allow him freedom to move in our midst as he wills. He will never abrogate the basic laws which he himself has embodied in the scriptures, though he may well do many things that will upset our own particular theological or traditional ideas. But after all, who is Lord of the church?

Such a renewing of our collective Christian mind would have a tremendously revitalizing effect on the church at large. It would also bring a new breath of life to multitudes of Christian women, particularly those who are single.

The single woman, then, finds herself in an imperfect church fellowship. Women in general are accorded inferior status, which all too many men have a vested interest in maintaining. Church activities are heavily oriented towards family life — right in itself, but a problem for some just the same. Once a single woman is past the age of belonging to the college and career group (usually 22, seldom more than 25), she is faced with a dilemma. She doesn't fit in anywhere. She can't attend the activities of the married couples' groups, although that is where most of her friends now are. The mission circles consist of women only, and are usually segregated according to marital status or lack of it. So again she may be arbitrarily separated from her friends; and she has no real choice as to programme or sphere of service. Occasionally, but not often, a church may offer mixed fellowship in some group other than the midweek prayer meeting or Bible study. Both will be taught by men (usually the same men year in, year out), and neither is likely to offer opportunity for meaningful discussion. The single woman who needs the normal give and take between men and women in a mixed fellowship group where all are free to take part, seldom finds it in her church.

There is still the choir, of course, and Sunday school teaching, the crèche, and sometimes youth work. But many churches restrict women to teaching other women and girls or pre-adolescent boys. Where they would get their workers if it were not for the selfless women who are willing to teach the word of God even under such untoward circumstances, I do not know. All honour to the women who continue to do so.

Though all too many churches muffle women and ignore their gifts, new freedoms of many kinds are being experienced in many churches today. Among them is a greater freedom for women and a truer recognition of their contribution. May the Spirit of God move onward in power and strength! Any true increase in our freedom must come from him alone. If we demand or fight for freedom we shall only lose what we have. But our God is a God of freedom; let him be known for what he is!

The single woman must share in the corporate worship, witness and work of the church because it is Christ's body. "The institutional church may not attract her," writes Linda Le Sourd in her address "The Single Woman and the Church",

> but she must not let its failures keep her away. God promises to meet our needs, and for her, that may be outside the church; yet she is to go to the church to serve. Let the single woman commit herself to the church, not for her own comfort and satisfaction, but because the church represents the totality and richness of the whole Body of Christ.

Where would the Christian church be today if it were not for its women, including its countless single women? Who have been its most faithful workers and carried its unseen burdens of prayer and sacrificial giving? Who have been its missionaries to the difficult and dangerous places of the earth?

Lest anyone think that I am painting a picture deliberately dark and unrealistic, let me give a startling illustration. InterVarsity Christian Fellowship's first Missionary

Conference, forerunner of all the Urbana Conventions, was held in Toronto in 1946. It has been repeated every third year since. Yet it was not until 1973 that a woman took her place among its speakers — and Elisabeth Elliot Leitch pioneered a new missionary field. IVCF is one of the freest and most biblical of all Christian organizations. Their leadership is godly and progressive. Their Urbana Conventions have had a profound effect upon missions worldwide. Yet twenty-seven years passed by before a woman addressed the students on that subject with which women, and mostly single women, have had by far more personal encounter than men, that of Christian mission. Let freedom ring!

The world at large pays little attention to its single people. Gail Sheehy, in the 550 pages of her book *Passages: The Predictable Crises of Adult Life* (Dutton, and Corgi paperback) investigates her subject thoroughly, going at length into one case history after another until it becomes difficult to differentiate between them. Yet she disposes of the never-married, both men and women, whom she estimates to number about 15% of all humanity, in half a dozen hasty paragraphs. Apparently we have no crises, predictable or otherwise; either that, or we are not adults. In any case, we don't signify. Warm thought to cheer the single heart on a frosty morning! This may be the world's view, but the church should have clearer vision.

It is true that Christian attention is focusing on the single person today more than it has in the past. Many large churches are appointing ministers to work exclusively among the single people of their congregations. This is good. But the concern does not appear to be with the needs of their never-married members so much as with their young people, their widowed, and with those whose marriages have broken up, leaving them alone, temporarily at least. This is worthy concern. These people need our help. But such a group does nothing for the true single person except to reinforce his feelings of being a non-person. He still doesn't exist in the eyes of his church. The new single people's groups may become, in effect, one more thing from which he feels excluded. Few churches could continue to function today if it were not for the gifts, both spiritual and temporal, of their single members. It is time their needs were recognized and true ministry was provided for them.

How is this to be done? The whole church can't be reorganized for the benefit of its single people! No, and it doesn't have to be. It merely needs to open all its doors to all its people, which it can do quite easily. What single people most need and want is to mingle naturally with others, men and women, single and married, in groups of their own choosing. They do not enjoy segregation. "Singles should be involved in the total church community where they can enjoy the diversity of the whole body of Christ."

Church activities should centre more around Christian fellowship, service and areas of special interest, and less around sex, age, or marital status. One minister I know refuses to have a couples' club in his church. He considers it discriminatory — a forward-looking man indeed! Instead, he has local fellowship groups meeting in homes in the various areas of his community. To these anyone is welcome.

Another church I know has zoned its congregation age-wise for its house meetings. Both single and married people belong to the group which roughly fits their own age decade, and they worship, study, serve and engage in chosen activities such as tenpin bowling, picnicking, etc., together. Some churches have house meetings because their facilities are limited; others because of the heightened freedom and fellowship a home can give.

Such grouping does not mean that there cannot be a meeting now and then devoted to some topic of particular interest to only some members of the group, such as parents wishing to discuss their needs concerning their children. But such meetings should not be the norm; and single people should neither absent themselves from them nor be excluded. In fact, many a single teacher, social worker, counsellor or doctor can help the parents in his group to understand their children better. For years I have addressed couples' clubs about such things. It seemed to me a sad anomaly that I was welcomed at their meetings when I was the speaker, and not when they had a psychiatrist or a probation officer whom I myself might be anxious to hear!

In many churches now, women are being welcomed to positions on official committees where marital status is not a consideration. Some women enjoy tough mental interaction with others more than they enjoy more usual activities. Working on committees can meet their personal needs as well as allow them to contribute a practical, useful point of view to the business matters of the church.

Few structural changes in the church's programme need be made to make single people feel that they really belong in the congregation, but certain changes in attitude must come about if single and married people are to find fellowship in mixed groups. Married women must conquer their inherent fear of single women and learn to trust them. Married men must get over the notion that single women are anxious for their attentions. And single people must prove themselves worthy of married trust. We must all learn to stand in transparent truth before God and before each other.

Single people are also going to have to take a good look in the mirror. They must stop complaining. They must stop feeling sorry for themselves. They must learn how to contribute positively to a group. They must do their share of the work, even if some of it is cooking, in which some single women may feel inferior to their more experienced sisters. They must learn to open their mouths and talk.

For we single people are often our own worst enemies. We want to belong to a group where leadership in discussion is passed around, but we don't want to take a turn. We want to sit under a good teacher in a Bible study, but we don't want to be that teacher, even occasionally. We want to enjoy a good discussion, but we don't want to contribute to it. In effect, we want to have our cake and eat it too.

A lecturer at a recent summer session at Regent College in Vancouver, a married man who carried on his heart a great burden for single people in the church, took time out of a busy teaching schedule to call an afternoon seminar on being single. He wanted to find out how single people feel about themselves, and how they think that their situation in the church can be improved. Single people turned up in droves. But when the meeting was thrown open for discussion, there was none. No one would talk. (It's easily seen I was not there!) Finally the meeting was adjourned. It might just as well never have been called.

It is easier to complain or to wallow in self-pity than it is to do something positive. Most single people are willing to do the first. Very few will attempt the second. Our problems will not be resolved until we do.

I should like to see the church do more for its single people. Perhaps one day things will be different. We should work and pray to that end. But change comes slowly. Meanwhile, if you are a single person who have honestly done all you can in your own church and still feel restricted, look around you. God has other branches of his church, and many kinds of service. If you are willing to take a risk and try something new or difficult, God will give you plenty to do and great joy and encouragement in doing it. Try helping in a mission or other Christian organization. Start a Bible study or prayer group in your home or place of work. Become a hospital visitor. Start a Bible club for the children in your neighbourhood. Develop some creative gift such as writing, music or other means of communication, and use it to communicate the gospel. You may be surprised where some such humble beginning may lead you. You may even end up writing a book on being single!

God is not bound. He has given all his children gifts to be used for the good of his whole body. No one is meant to be idle. If one avenue of service seems impenetrable, ask God to lead you to another. Then serve him with all your heart.

Open Letter To A Married Friend

Dear Rosemary:

Ever since getting back from my visit to you I have wanted to tell you just how much that weekend in your home meant to me. Yet how can I tell you what I can hardly find words to say?

It's just over fifteen years now since you and I left school and went to work in the heart of the city. For a few years it was fun to live in bedsitters not far from each other, to work and plan and dream together, and to be busy in the Lord's work. Our furnished rooms were all the home that either of us had. When Jim came into your life, I was so glad for you, and I hoped that in his own good time God would give me what he had given you. I hoped that I, too, might share in the building of a truly Christian home — a place whose doors would ever be open in Christ's service.

Fifteen years have passed since then, and God has not seen fit to fulfil my desires. You and Jim married and had your family. I am still living in a city bedsitter, trying to make a home for myself on what time and strength a working girl has left after the necessities of life and the exactitudes of a heavy teaching schedule are cared for.

It's pretty uphill work — and unutterably lonely.

Don't get me wrong, Rosemary — I'm not feeling sorry for myself. I know that single girls have a freedom and certain advantages that you married folk don't have, and that God has much work to be done that only we can do. I know, too, that he will fill and satisfy with his very self the empty hearts and lives that we bring to him. He has done this for me, and for countless other single women I know; and I am happy in him. But oh, Rosemary, you can not imagine how much it meant to spend last week end in a home instead of a tiny room, and to cuddle your darling baby!

You know, it's a funny thing, and probably you have never noticed it, but most married girls seem to drop their single friends after a few years of marriage. I suppose it's only natural, since our interests and viewpoints do gradually diverge; and of course it's easier for couples to do things with other couples, especially if there are children. But it eventually comes to mean that we single girls are thrown entirely on each other for companionship — and since most of us live in bedsitters, that means that we never have any contact with home life. I could count on the fingers of one hand the number of times I've spent an evening or a Sunday in a home in the last six months. Oh, yes, I'm busy, and I have lots of friends — grand girls, all of them. We go to church activities, and to concerts and lectures; and of course there are the inevitable dinners in restaurants. Good dinners, too, and no responsibility for getting them or clearing up afterwards. But I'd trade the best of them for the soup and crackers we had in your kitchen, with the children in their pyjamas and dressing gowns, and stories and cocoa by the fire afterwards. And then family prayers and tuck-me-up time — those wide, wondering eyes, and little clinging arms and warm, sweet, goodnight kisses ....

Probably you married folk never stop to think that what has come to be merely routine to you can be a song to remember for us. I suppose that bedtime seven nights a week becomes commonplace, a pleasurable enough though sometimes unruly little chore that often interferes with other things you'd like to do, and makes it awkward to entertain guests to dinner — especially single girls who can't understand the suppertime pressures on a busy mother.

But I wish my other married friends had the same deep wisdom that you have, Rosemary, to know that what makes us happy and warmly grateful is not to be "entertained" beautifully in a perfectly kept lounge, but to be allowed to share in the ordinary activities of a normal home — busy, perhaps noisy, even a bit disrupted in spots, but richly human; and oh, so enjoyable to a girl who has no home! You let me wash up — how often do I have the opportunity to wash pretty china? You let me bathe the baby — and we both live to tell the tale! You let me cut flowers for the table, and set the logs a-crackling in the fireplace. I haven't sat by an open fire since I was at your place last Christmas, and I can't remember when I was last turned loose in a garden. And it was such fun to help you prepare the vegetables for dinner, while we got caught up on six months' backlog of chatter, and the kettle sang and the kitten purred and the old Dutch clock kept time with its ridiculous off-key ticking. Of course, you know me so well that you know I would far sooner peel potatoes and chat in the kitchen than sit formally in a living room anywhere. But what I can't understand is why more married girls don't realize that most single friends are simply heart-hungry for just such titbits of home life as they could so easily spare — that our interests and viewpoints aren't nearly as divergent as they may think. Then maybe they'd stop feeling that they had to "fuss" if they asked us to dinner, and let us visit them a little more often. Chances are that they would find as much pleasure in such fellowship as we would.

Well, we both had our dreams fifteen years ago, and I'm glad that yours have come true. You and Jim have really realized your ideal of a Christian home, and have made your home a veritable Bethany to numberless souls. It can't have been easy, for a minister's wife has very little life of her own, and you've had little enough to come and go on, and a fair share of trouble and illness. But you've shown that when hearts are willing to share, God will make his well of blessing to spring up. I believe you have been blessed yourselves in sharing your happiness with others, and you have passed on your vision of what Christian home life should be to ever so many young couples in your congregation. I think that God has probably used your home to bless others just as much as he has used Jim's preaching—maybe more. That is a service that every Christian housewife could render if she would. I wish more of them realized it.

It will be ages before I can get to see you again—wish you didn't live so far away! But in the meantime, thanks again for all your love and understanding. Good night, and God's blessing on you all. Give the baby an extra kiss for me!

Love, Margaret

"Open Letter To My Married Sister" from Christian Life magazine, Illinois.

Letter To A Friend

Dear Jane:

Your letter written on Joan's wedding day arrived yesterday, and I've thought of it almost continually since. I know how it feels to be bridesmaid at a younger sister's wedding, and I appreciate your honesty in describing your mixed emotions.

All of us have to face the possibility that God's plan for our lives may not include marriage, and of course you wonder if there can ever be complete victory over your natural desire for a husband, a home and children. I'll try, since you ask me, to share with you some of the ways in which God has directed my thinking along these lines.

The fact that you're now 25 and not married does not necessarily mean that marriage is not in God's plan for you. God may have someone for you whom he has not yet brought into your life. But I believe that you're wise to recognize the possibility of having to spend your life alone, and to face it: to bring this part of your life to him in complete surrender. You'll find it's not something achieved overnight or arrived at easily; yet the sooner we begin to bring this innermost core of our lives to God in utter relinquishment, the easier it will be to learn the secret of real victory, not only in this area, but in all others. I'm sure it's not possible to know true victory along general lines if one has not at least begun to seek and to find his victory in this most difficult and important question.

We don't know why God chooses to give the joys of marriage to some of his children and to withhold them from others, and at first there's a tendency to feel left out, almost cheated of something that is ours by right. It is hard to look at other Christians who have what we lack and not ask "Why?"

This painful "Why?" must be brought to God in surrender over and over again as life goes on. Indeed, there is no answer to it on earth. How non-Christians, especially girls, deal with such problems I can't imagine. I'm profoundly thankful that I am not in this position.

But for us who have committed our lives to God through Jesus Christ, there is an answer, and in it is peace. We know that in God's infinite wisdom and sovereignty, his way is perfect, and that one radiant morning in the light of his eternal revelation all such questions will be answered to our utmost satisfaction. How thankful I am that I know him! Sometimes I try to imagine what it would be like to face life without him. Oh, Jane, what a wonderful thing it is to know Jesus Christ!

Now supposing that God is calling you to a single life, how can you face it without becoming bitter, frustrated and resentful?

First, of course, as I've already said, you must bring all of your life to God in unconditional surrender, and especially this part with its details and implications. Then you must seek to grow along certain lines that will help make his victory really yours.

I think perhaps it's here that some Christian girls fail. Accepting the possibility that they will remain unmarried, they either consciously or unconsciously assume that as a result only a second-best life is open to them, and accordingly they live on the plains instead of finding the wings that God would provide for soaring to the heights. For the mountain peaks of Christian living aren't reserved for the married alone. They are reachable to all who want to appropriate his grace to scale them. And sometimes I think that he has special heights of joy in himself for those from whom he has withheld the beauties of marriage.

That true Christian marriage is beautiful, no one can deny. It is the highest expression on earth of the relationship between Christ and his church. To look at it scornfully and say, in effect, "I didn't want that anyway", is to disparage God's loveliest revelation of himself outside Christ. Too many single girls adopt this sour grapes attitude, but the path to victory doesn't run through that vineyard. We shouldn't be ashamed of our natural desire for marriage, which is God-given and right. But neither should we feel that, lacking such consummation, our lives will be incomplete. For we are complete in Jesus Christ, and the most beautiful marriage on earth is only a shadow of that union with him which may be experienced by any one who will earnestly set herself to seek it.

I sometimes wonder if God has withheld marriage from me so that my whole heart may be centred on love for him. If so, I have "the better part", for to know him is the truest satisfaction in life. Not that married people may not or do not know this; many of God's greatest saints have been married. But I can't help noticing the amazing heights reached by certain unmarried women (Amy Carmichael, Mary Slessor, Frances Ridley Havergal, to name a few) and to wonder, at least, if a special fulness of joy and achievement may not be reserved for the unmarried woman who seeks to give herself, soul and body, to the Lord Jesus Christ. I wonder if it is by accident that the names of countless single women are among the greatest in missionary history, or if it may be for reasons something like this. But I'm digressing ....

I think that most, perhaps all, of the highest joys of marriage are open to the soul who knows Christ; and to know him in his fulness must be the supreme desire of our lives.

The companionship and fellowship of a God-given marriage are a lovely thing. One is never alone for very long. In absence the partners experience a sweet sense of each other's presence, an overwhelming desire for the beloved one's return. But this is merely a picture, a shadow of the relationship between Christ and his own, of which we may have the very substance. As we realize more and more of his presence, we come to know that we, too, are never alone. Though absent from him now, our hearts rest in his sweet companionship, and more and more earnestly long for the hour of his return. Death becomes our entrance to his beloved presence.

And these things are not theory. They are reality — the quintessence of Christian experience, as real as marriage itself. They are real enough to take away the chill of entering an empty flat when you come home from work, real enough to fill lonely evenings with exquisite content. Are they even more real than a companion in the flesh? I do not know; I only know that the companionship of Jesus is real and satisfying. And you may find this reality, too, if you come to him for it.

Perhaps you've longed for the mutual understanding that God gives to the man and woman he has brought together. Though one's closest friends may misunderstand, one's life partner, if the marriage was made in heaven, seldom will. You and I can substitute for that "seldom" an indisputable "never". The infinite understanding of the Son of God penetrates every part of our lives, going far beyond that of the most loving and discerning husband, far beyond our understanding of ourselves. What rest, what serenity, what security is ours in him! Every human being longs for another's complete understanding; comparatively few achieve it, even in the sweetest marriage ties. Yet it is ours for the taking. God has not withheld this priceless gift from us just because we are not married. Let us cultivate it, living in its beauty.

Another joy of marriage not denied us is the expression of our love in service. How eagerly the Christian wife tries to please her husband, preparing his favourite dishes, keeping their home clean and neat and his washing lovingly and carefully done, endeavouring to fill his leisure hours with joy and content, seeking fittingly to entertain his business associates. All this opportunity is ours, and more. To make our hearts a worthy and spotless home for our beloved, yielding ourselves to him who himself works this within us by his Spirit; to seek to please him in the tiniest details of our lives; to delight his heart with our love and praise and companionship; to serve his church because it brings him joy: has any bride a higher and lovelier calling? And the rewards of such service are ours not only today, but through eternity.

What about children? I can hear you ask, for I know how you love them. Surely, you will say, this is one place where only marriage can satisfy the deep longing of every woman to bring other lives into the world, to love and nurture them, to bring them up to know and serve the Saviour. Surely this is one thing denied the woman who does not marry.

On the contrary, Jane, this is a sphere in which we may be as productive as our married sisters, possibly more so, since we shall probably have more time over the years than they. The unmarried woman in union with Christ will know, richly and abundantly, the joy of creating new life in fellowship with him. He desires that we bring forth fruit unto eternal life; and if we yield ourselves to him, he will fulfil his good pleasure through us, and we shall know the holy joys of spiritual motherhood.

Recently I spent a week's holiday with an old school friend who has just recently become a Christian. I have seldom seen such hunger for the things of God. We spent every available moment discussing spiritual things and in prayer and fellowship. How she drank in the things of Christ! I was utterly drained after each long talk, yet exquisitely happy and content! During that beautiful week I wondered if any human mother nursing her child ever knew more joy and satisfaction than I in nurturing this newly-born soul.

The unmarried woman who has learned to share the life of the Son of God will be able to give to others in their time of need. Not long ago a young friend of mine lost her baby and I tried to comfort her. Evidently what I had to say touched her heart, for she burst out: "*How* can you understand so well? I don't see how anyone who hasn't been through it can possibly know what it's like to lose your baby, but you really seem to know! How can you do it?" I smiled, and murmured something conventional. What I could have told her was that any single woman who has relinquished all claims to married happiness and given them back to God has known the death of not one but all her children, of her husband, her home, of all such hopes and dreams. She has indeed "been through it", and can enter another's sorrow and bring the comfort wherewith she herself has been comforted by God.

We must remember too, Jane, that not all marriages bring these joys of companionship, fellowship and understanding. Not all wives find love's reward in service. Many are lonely, misunderstood, and serve all their lives for meagre thanks. Not all wives become mothers, and of those who do, not all see their children find eternal life in Christ. Surely this must be among the greatest of all sorrows.

But for the woman who finds her all in Jesus Christ, satisfaction in all these things is assured. Fellowship and love transcending even the most beautiful human relationship is ours if we will have it. Spiritual motherhood is certain if we know Christ aright, and none of our children will ever be lost to him.

But are there no regrets? Is it possible always to live in the realm of the spiritual? Have we not physical bodies with physical needs that make themselves felt?

In the first place, no one has to make the sacrifices involved in remaining single all at once. Fortunately, we can't see into the future, and day by day there are lovely, absorbing, satisfying experiences. Our work, friendships, recreation, hobbies, Christian service all help. Life today for the healthy intelligent single woman can be very rewarding. If we had to meet all our problems at once or without aid, we might indeed be overwhelmed.

As the years go by, however, deep insistent voices make themselves heard within us. This undertone can be very strong and it grows with the years. But if we have been living in fellowship with God, our life in him has been growing too; and if we have trusted him in this matter early in life and renewed our commitment whenever a new surge of desire or loneliness has arisen, we find that his answer not only keeps pace with these inner questionings, but actually transcends them. At least that has been my experience. It is infinitely easier for me to be single today than it was twenty or even ten years ago. This is not because the human heart becomes less lonely as the years pass — it becomes more so — but my fellowship with Christ is so much deeper now that the voices of loneliness are heard less clearly, even though humanly speaking they may be louder.

A great deal depends upon entering this committed relationship with Christ long before it becomes evident that you are likely to remain unmarried. That's why I'm writing you in such detail. Seek his grace *now* in this regard. If you marry, this union with Christ will be your greatest assurance of a happy marriage; if you don't marry, it is your only security against a lonely, bitter, barren old age.

Of course there will always be difficulties. Desires you had thought completely committed will suddenly arise to stab you at unexpected times. A child's face, a fleeting exchange of tender glances between a wife and her husband when you are visiting, a new bride's radiance — such things may catch you unawares with a swelling of desire that will be very strong. But don't waste time worrying about them. Such desires are not wrong, but they must continually be kept under his control. At such moments renew your commitment to him, seek his grace, lift your heart to him in love and trust, and he will fill it with himself.

I have found that one of the hardest things about being alone is that when a sudden surge of affection wells up within me, as it does in every normal outgoing woman, there is no one on whom to bestow it. Oh, I know the books say to go visit a hospital, help some needy child and so on; these things of course are helpful. But if you are at home, alone, with no time to go out seeking those who need your love just then, you can be almost swamped by the power of that need to give affection — and what can you do? I have found perfect and beautiful release by simply and deliberately lifting my heart in a flood of adoration to God, pouring out my soul before him in worship and praise. His answering infilling of love and contentment is instantaneous, overwhelming in its power and beauty.

Does he let these deep desires spring up within us in order that we may satisfy our hearts with his love and his heart with ours? I think he does. To know that we may bring joy to the heart of God is a solemn and wonderful thing. Oh, Jane, there is no longing that he cannot fill, for he calls those whom he asks to walk alone on earth to a moment-by-moment, continuous life of love and fellowship with him.

Such a life has its rewards not only on earth but also in heaven. There every soul will know perfect and complete happiness as each is filled with the fulness of God. But we can only be filled to capacity; souls of great capacity will know more of God than souls of lesser capacity. The closeness of our fellowship with Christ on earth determines our capacity for eternal enjoyment of him. The more time and thought and love we give him now, the richer and deeper and fuller shall be our experience of God in eternity. May he teach us to use every opportunity for his eternal glory and our eternal good!

I like to remember that our Lord Jesus was unmarried. Although he was the Son of God, he had a human body just as we have. His humanity would have been incomplete had not he too known the pull of physical desire. We catch a glimpse of his longing for companionship in his cry to the disciples, "Will ye also go away?" and we see something of his desire for home life in his enjoyment of the home at Bethany. I am sure that the Son of man must have longed for someone of his own, just as we do. He found his answer in fellowship with God; there is no other answer. When we read that he was in every respect tempted as we are, yet without sinning, and is able to help those who are tempted, we realize that he knows and understands our fear of not marrying and all its implications. He is ready to give us his companionship and victory if we come to him.

We must never forget that his love for us is so great that he was willing to forgo his perfect fellowship with the Father, suffering the darkness of utter and complete loneliness, that we might know the joys of fellowship with God. Surely he who loved us unto death will not withhold the comfort of his fellowship from those who need and seek it!

God lead you in his way and keep you in his love.

Lovingly, Margaret.

"If You Don't Marry" from HIS magazine, 1958.

Helpful Books To Read

C. S. Lewis, *The Four Loves* (Collins/Fount).
James Olthuis, *I Pledge You My Troth* (Harper & Row).
Ada Lum, *Single And Human* (InterVarsity Press).
Margaret Evening, *Who Walk Alone* (Hodder & Stoughton).
John White, *Eros Defiled* (InterVarsity Press).
John White, *The Fight* (InterVarsity Press).
Dorothy Pape, *In Search of God's Ideal Woman* (InterVarsity Press).
Elisabeth Elliot, *Let Me Be A Woman* (Tyndale House Publishers).
C. S. Lewis, *The Problem of Pain* (Collins/Fount).
Alex Davidson, *The Returns of Love* (InterVarsity Press).